olf Moon • Snow Moon • Death Moon • Pink Moon • Flower Moon

For Edyta and Sue, for their unwavering belief in me

Crumps Barn Studio
Syde, Cheltenham GL53 9PN
www.crumpsbarnstudio.co.uk

Copyright © Amaris Chase 2024

The right of Amaris Chase to be identified as the author of this work has been asserted in accordance with the Copyright, Designs and Patents Act 1988.

All rights reserved. No part of this publication may be reproduced, stored in a retrieval system, or transmitted in any form or by any means, electronic, mechanical, photocopying, recording or otherwise, without the prior permission of the copyright owner.

Blood Moon previously published in *Spooky Ambiguous (Crumps Barn Studio 2022)*
Werewoof previously published as *Vampire Cat* in *Festival of Cats (Crumps Barn Studio 2022)*, newly revised and updated in this edition

Cover design and illustrations by Lorna Gray © 2024

Typeset in Adobe Garamond Pro

All our books are printed on responsibly sourced paper from managed woodlands and recycled material. Printed in the UK by TJ Books, Padstow

ISBN 978-1-915067-42-5

se Moon • Thunder Moon • Red Moon • Harvest Moon • Hunter's M

DARK MOON TALES

AMARIS CHASE

Crumps Barn Studio

JANUARY • **WOLF MOON** • *7*
The Keeper • Ice Maidens

FEBRUARY • **SNOW MOON** • *23*
Unwanted Guest • Eternal Magic

MARCH • **DEATH MOON** • *35*
Séance of the Damned • The Confession

APRIL • **PINK MOON** • *47*
Monster Date • Kitchen God • Leerie

MAY • **FLOWER MOON** • *67*
Ghost Marriage • Double Take

JUNE • **ROSE MOON** • *79*
The Keening • The Magic Carpet

JULY • **THUNDER MOON** • *93*
Come To Me • The Shadow

AUGUST • **RED MOON** • *105*
Resurrected • Honesty • The Spell Consultant

SEPTEMBER • **HARVEST MOON** • *123*
Unwanted Guest • No Hiding Place

OCTOBER • **HUNTER'S MOON** • *141*
Godcake • Werewoof • Blood Moon

NOVEMBER • **FROST MOON** • *161*
The Scrying Game • You Don't Belong Here

DECEMBER • **COLD MOON** • *185*
A Gift from the Magi • G-Hosts

LUNAR ECLIPSE • **BLOOD MOON** *195*
Blood Donor • Blood Moon – The prelude

JANUARY

WOLF MOON

THE KEEPER

*"You don't find them,
They find you"*

ELIZABETH SHIVERED, and not just from the biting wind, as she thought back to her grandfather's warning when she was a child, sitting on his lap by the coal fire, inhaling the smoke from his pipe. He used to tell her tales of fairies, goblins and dragons, but the tale of these unseen people was different. He was adamant that they existed. He had sought them out deliberately, but he refused to elaborate why or even how he had found them. Now, years later when she was a grandparent herself, she understood why her grandfather had told her the tale. She also wanted to find the unseen. A bark from her dog brought her mind sharply back to the present. Her dog looked at her expectantly. She strengthened her resolve to go through with her mission.

There is a bond between a human and their dog, where the dog understands what the human is thinking without being spoken to. Dogs sense fear, happiness, agitation, and sometimes read thoughts. It was through this bond that Elizabeth and her dog were tentatively walking through the forest at the edge of the town. "Keep looking," Elizabeth stroked her dog in encouragement. The dog threw her a look as if to say, "Are you sure?" She gave him a slight nod, trying not to show her fear but knew full well that her faithful companion could sense it in her.

The dog scampered through bracken, ivy and the detritus of foliage that had receded for winter. The deeper they went into the thicket, the more frightened Elizabeth became. Shadows seemed to follow her, the trees looked like they were watching her, waiting … maybe they knew the secret she was seeking.

The moon offered little light beneath the lattice of branches. The further they went into the forest, the more alert she became to the sense of unease that slowly crept through her bones. She felt there was someone right up against her back, almost breathing on her neck. Elizabeth kept looking behind her only to be met by the mocking darkness. They must be near now, she thought. Then her spine felt like a jolt of electricity had shot through it. The air thickened around her, crackling with anticipation, a foreboding sense of harm to come her way. Her instincts warned her to turn around and run back to the safety of her home. It felt like a barrier, an evil presence to protect the creatures from being discovered.

The dog stopped abruptly, his tail erect in warning. He started growling at something ahead. "What is it boy?" Elizabeth needed to break the silence. She scanned ahead but couldn't see anything of note at first, until she saw a flash of white up a slope behind the trees. This was it, this was what she had been looking for.

Reluctantly she turned to her dog. "Home! Now!"

The dog gave a short bark in protest.

"Go!" she insisted and watched her faithful companion slink reproachfully away until his silhouette had been subsumed in the darkness. She swallowed hard and climbed up the slope. There was an ancient wall she had never seen before, It was covered in a thick layer of moss, and then she saw the flash of white again …

There was a hole in the wall. Her breathing became shallow, she heard her heart beat at an alarming rate. She was too frightened to go through with this now. She had never felt so alone. She shut her eyes so she didn't have to look at her fate, and then she gasped in pain as the malignant part of her reminded her why she was risking everything this January night. She gritted her teeth and crawled through the hole. There was more forest on the other side, but the figure in white was waiting for her. It was the figure of a white wolf.

It stared at her. As with her dog, she felt an intuitive connection. She needed to follow him, he would not harm her. He turned around and started walking, stopping every now and then to check that she was still following. Eventually they came to a break in the forest, not exactly a clearing, but a mass of ivy and fallen branches. A lone yew tree stood on one side and a thick mist hung over the ground. The mist lifted slowly, almost deliberately and revealed fragments of granite breaking though the ivy. She realised the ivy was just a camouflage. This was a circle of headstones with a yew tree forming part of the circumference.

Elizabeth was too scared to do anything other than breathe.

The mist turned black, gathered in the centre and swirled and flowed and solidified into a figure of a woman. Elizabeth swallowed hard. She had been expecting … expecting what? A thin and towering figure in a cape? A woman in a white nightdress? She had been conditioned by the stereotypical images from the films of her youth.

"So you have found us. You are in the company of the few …" The voice was low and seductive. Elizabeth tried to make out the figure in the darkness. Her head was shorn of its hair, her skin gleamed like mahogany in the moonlight. Elizabeth couldn't help frowning. The woman gave a deep, throaty laugh. "Not what you were expecting? My breed transcends race and cultures. That's just your perception of what I should be."

"I … I'm sorry …!" Elizabeth stammered in shame. How could she be so racist?

"Don't be, I like the shock factor." The woman grinned to reveal her sharpened teeth. Elizabeth gasped. Then she heard a growl and looked down to see a terrier at the feet of the lady. It bared its teeth at her, also revealing fangs.

"It's OK," said the woman, but not reassuringly, "He won't bite … Unless I tell him to …" She laughed at her own joke, then abruptly stopped and gave Elizabeth an icy stare. "How did you find us?"

Elizabeth had to push her fear down, she was here for a purpose. "My dog … I used my dog."

"Hmmm. Clever, I thought the spirits would have made you turn back."

"The spirits?" Elizabeth was curious despite her fear.

"The spirits in the woods, before the wall. You can't see them, but they gather around intruders until they are overcome by such a strong sense of danger and dread that they subconsciously choose a different direction away from the trees. The spirits have kept animals and humans away for years. Your dog must be exceptional."

"He's not afraid to face his fears."

"And neither are you," The woman smiled, but it was devoid of warmth. "I am Kamauri. I am the keeper of this lair." She looked at Elizabeth expectantly, as if she knew the request was coming.

Elizabeth's heart beat violently, but curiosity got the better of her. This woman didn't fit the mould of her image of the undead. "How did you come to be here? Are there others?" She immediately regretted her question, she shouldn't be so inquisitive! She had come so far and could lose it all now through her own stupidity! But Kamauri smiled at her indulgently, almost pleased to tell her story.

"We travelled on a merchant ship to trade with the local villages here. They didn't understand what we were. They captured us but they didn't have the knowledge at the time of how to destroy us – but they understood witchcraft and the power of the circle." Kamauri shuddered and winced at the memory. "They buried us in a circle knowing that we would be trapped, and planted a yew tree between the graves thinking it would ward off evil. But the yew only works with spirits. We were forgotten about over time, but through the years a few headstones collapsed and the circle was broken. We were finally released after decades of sleep!

"We stay as a small group, we don't make ourselves known to the villagers. We prey on animals and humans who will not be missed. The spirits in the forest stop people from coming near us with the presence they create. Most people turn away, but *you* broke through the barrier."

Kamauri studied her curiously. "You must be desperate to get this far. Why have you come?"

Now here was the crux of the matter, but Elizabeth was speechless again, this time from emotional pain. She struggled to say it out loud, even to family. She opened her mouth, and closed it silently as tears welled up and rolled down her cheek in a steady stream.

Kamauri smiled at her, again displaying her needlepoint teeth, then she took Elizabeth's hand and caressed it gently with her own smooth, icy hand to stimulate the circulation. Elizabeth stood mesmerised, and then suddenly yelped, "Ouch!" as Kamurai abruptly brought the finger to her lips and punctured it tantalisingly with a fang and squeezed the finger lightly until the warm blood gushed out. Kamauri licked the finger slowly and lasciviously, her tongue felt like cold glass against Elizabeth's skin. ,

Elizabeth stood petrified, was the moment that she has been waiting for about to come?

Kamauri frowned. "I know this blood, I have tasted something similar before ... the old man! You are related to him ... Let me see ... He was here too long ago to be your father ... Your grandfather maybe?"

"Yes," affirmed Elizabeth, astonished at Kamauri's memory of her grandfather through the blood. "He told me he had found you, but he didn't say why he looked for you, or what you had said."

"He came for the same reason you have come. I can taste the malignancy in your blood, as I did in his."

"I only have 6 months left to live. A year at the most. I can't bear to leave my family. It's too early for me to leave them, I want to see my grandchildren grow up. I feel cheated by life." How could she explain? Would Kamauri have the emotions to understand?

"Then I will tell you what I told your grandfather: Becoming one of us is not what you think. You don't feel about people the way you do in life. You will not feel love for your family."

"I will never stop loving my family, in life or death. That love will never leave me," replied Elizabeth defiantly.

Kamauri suppressed a smile. "As you wish. As you have found us, I should honour your achievement by fulfilling your request. Go back home now, the wolf will lead you back, we will come for you at the right time. "

"Won't you do it now?"

"If we do it here, your body will never be found. We will do it in the village, when you least expect it. We are less likely to raise attention that way."

Elizabeth nodded ascent. The wolf growled. It was time to leave. "Thank you," she muttered and turned to leave. She couldn't help turning back to take a last look at Kamauri, who stood exactly where she had been with her terrier by her side, and behind them were other shadow figures.

Elizabeth turned back around quickly. She didn't want to know the faces of the shadows, she didn't want to keep looking out for them.

I found them, Grandpa! she thought, as she finally reached the cottage she had inherited from her grandfather, filled with special memories of the time shared with him the kind of memories that she wanted to pass on to her own grandchildren now. She fancied she could smell the distinct aroma of her Grandfather's pipe as sat in his old rocking chair.

This time the scent of the pipe was bitter, almost

disapproving. "I had to do it, Grandpa," she said resolutely.

A FEW MONTHS LATER, a little girl woke up with the moonlight caressing her face. She clutched her teddy as she noticed the shadow in the window. She wanted to scream but was too frightened. There was a tapping on the window, and a familiar voice. "Let me in my darling!"

In a daze, the girl walked up to the window.

"Grandma? What are you doing outside? Mummy said you were in heaven!"

"Let me in, my darling, it's so cold out here! I've come from heaven to visit you! Don't you want to see your Grandma again?"

The girl opened the latch tentatively. The figure pulled open the window violently and the girl gasped and stepped back. The figure barely noticed the look of horror on the girl's face, and proceeded to envelop the girl in a cold embrace. "Hello my darling, I missed you," said the figure, nuzzling the girl's neck …

ICE MAIDENS

"THESE ARE THE houses built on the old incinerator plan." My friend Adrienne indicated to uniform blocks of flats overlooking woodlands.

"They must smell nice then," I said, attempting some humour. This was difficult for me. I am what some would politely class as 'different'. Not quite autistic, but certainly I was often in a world of my own, and couldn't relate to the 'normal' world. Adrienne accepted this, one of the few who did. She had kindly elected to give me a tour of the town following my move up to her city after accepting a post at the University.

Adrienne was taking great delight in showing off her knowledge of local history whilst walking her black Labrador who, given the weather, was aptly named Misty. We followed a muddy track covered in autumn leaves down to a tunnel covered in incongruous pink graffiti, and emerging on the other side to a tranquil pond with ducks swimming playfully in umber coloured water. I was not good with emotions, but I had a soft spot for watching birds, especially aquatic ones. We walked to the edge of the bank. I stared at the reflections of the trees on the other side.

"You would think this is such a peaceful spot, wouldn't you? In fact, this is the local suicide spot," said Adrienne flatly.

"Here? Why here?" I asked incredulously.

"Folklore has it that this is where witches were dunked. That some of their pain remains here, and draws others who are in emotional pain."

"Or perhaps because it's the only pond in the area?" I asked, my scientific mind trying to process this information.

"Or that," agreed Adrienne. "But the odd thing is, it is mostly men who take their own life here. There must be easier ways to kill yourself than to drown yourself."

"Rationality isn't a strong point of someone depressed," I pointed out. Adrienne nodded her head in agreement.

Misty looked into the water and started growling. "She's afraid of her own reflection this one," grumbled Adrienne, whilst tugging at the dog. "Come on Misty!" She turned to me and said with a mischievous smile, "Now I'll take you to the spot where the witches were burned.". I smiled back, and turned to leave, but not before I took a last glance at the ducks. It was then that I noticed her, just the reflection at first, the girl with the blonde hair and long white dress, her figure distorted as the water gently rippled her reflection. I looked to the bank on the other side, but no one was there. I looked again at the water, and it had returned to the same murky brown. I shook my head and gave myself a mental admonishment at my terrible imagination.

Autumn turned to winter. I regularly walked down that woodland path in all weathers, it cleared my mind, distracted me, and helped me find solutions to problems. My mind was wired for mathematics. I did not see beauty in the same way as you might do. I saw beauty in shapes, the factorials in leaves, the geometry of flowers, the twists of branches in trees. I would always stop at the pond to view the ducks.

On one crisp morning, I saw her again at the other side of the pond. She stood barefoot at the edge of the pond, her hair lifting in undulations by the wind. At the back of my mind, the frequency of the oscillations of the hair was being calculated, that it took a few moments for me to wonder about her bare feet and the inappropriate white summer dress given the weather. I was about to cry out to her, ask her if she needed help, but she just held out her arms and smiled at me, and then turned around and ran off into the trees on the other side. I could have chased her but there was no way to cross the pond that quickly, I would have to circumnavigate the pond. I rationalised that some people enjoy the cold weather, taking dips in ponds in winter on the premise it revitalised the body. I was not keen on being rejuvenated in that manner and preferred a coffee in my mornings to perk me up. I puzzled over this encounter for a short while but then pushed it aside as some mathematical puzzle overtook my mind. Occasionally, the girl with the blonde hair and white summer dress came to mind, the puzzle being who was she and why was she dressed like that in cold weather, and barefoot. But I shook her out of my mind's eye as soon as I could. There was something about her image which made my skin crawl, but I had no rational explanation.

Christmas came, I spent it alone happily in my flat. I was more of a scrooge, not enjoying the festive atmosphere but happy for the enforced break. I enjoyed reading books on history, new mathematical theories, watching documentaries, doing puzzles. And my walks, I loved my daily walks away from the ever constant Christmas songs radiating out from all the shops and clashing with huge shopping bags. January was like an anti-climax, and February seemed to be the apex of winter, when snowstorms came and the pond iced over. My daily walk became treacherous with ice being my foe. I was never good with keeping my balance on ice, and was petrified of falling. On a particularly bright morning, with the ice not yet melted, I managed to get to the pond with a few near falls. I stopped to breathe in the chilled air, feeling it cleanse my head. The pond had iced over, a few ducks were waddling on it with as much grace as I myself had walking on ice. And then I saw her ... beneath the water this time. Her eyes bulged in panic, she was beating her fists against the ice, her hair fanned out like a halo. I took a moment to take this in. How could she be trapped beneath the ice? And then I saw her in that summer dress, her mouth make the shape of an 'O' as the water claimed her and she began to sink, her arms outstretched towards me as they had when I had seen her stand at the other side of the bank.

At last my brain clicked into action and I reached for a nearby stone to try and break the ice. It splintered and cracked after a few thrashes, and suddenly I felt an icy had grip mine ... she was still alive!!! I tried to grasp her hand and pull, but she was pulling me! 'No!' I cried in a panic! 'No! You're pulling me in!"

I don't know what came first, the shock from entering the cold water, or the shock that she was deliberately pulling me in. And as I sank into the murky depths of the water, I saw her smile gleefully at me, and I found myself surrounded by other girls, hands held and slowly rotating in a circle around me, in a corkscrew motion as I sank further. It dawned on me that these were the women who were dunked and drowned as witches, and who were luring men to their death ever since in revenge. Somewhere at the back of my mind, I did a calculation of my chances of survival with the supernatural against me ...

FEBRUARY

SNOW MOON

UNWANTED GUEST

"ALRIGHT! ALRIGHT! Hold your horses, I'm coming!" Katrina shouted at the vacant room as she dusted flour off her hands and onto her apron. She heard her husband's footsteps descending the stairs. The banging of the inn door continued relentlessly, urgently. She reached the door at last and unchained and unbolted it.

"Don't you know we're shut at …" she began angrily, but then as she drew open the door and saw what stood before her, she covered her mouth to stifle a scream.

"Katrina! Who is it?" her husband shouted behind her. He saw her turn and look at him with eyes wide open in horror, blood drained from her face. Stormy winds blew in through the open door and made Katrina's dress billow almost indecently.

Confused, Frederich opened the door wider to see who had affected his wife in such a terrible manner. Then he saw the figure within the doorframe, snow blowing and swirling like the furies behind it, and his face contorted into a look of shock too. He grabbed his wife by her shoulders, seemingly to protect her, but in reality he wanted to put her between him and the entity before them, and protect himself.

"Friederich! It can't be!" His wife finally broke the tense silence.

"It is, Katrina! He must have escaped. Otherwise how else could he be here? It is daylight, he could not have walked here in daylight if he was …" Friedrich left the sentence unfinished. Then he took command of the situation.

"Katrina! Quick, light the fire and bring him some ale. Come in, come in my good man! You must be frozen to the bone walking in this snowstorm …" Friedrich tried to lead the figure in the doorway in by the arm but the man shook him off roughly and walked in. He stared at Katrina, mouth set downwards. She felt his rage before she saw his gaze. She lit the grate and escaped to the kitchen as quickly as she could.

"Please, take a seat by the fire." Friedrich gestured to the man to take a prime seat by the warmth of the hearth. The man turned to him, still fuming, but seemingly unaffected by the cold, given that he wore only a shirt and waistcoat, and had no overcoat. He must have hypothermia by now.

"Katrina! The ale, quick!" Friedrich shouted towards the kitchen, and took a seat opposite the man.

Katrina shuffled in with a tankard of ale and quickly set it on the table beside the man. His eyes locked with hers, she sensed only evil and she fled back to the kitchen.

"Excuse my wife, such fragile nerves," said Friedrich in an attempt to bond with the man through a shared disdain for the female temperament. The man just looked at him with the same simmering fury.

"Look, I'm sorry about last night. We had to do it to protect ourselves you see," explained Friedrich nervously. The silence that hung between them could only be broken by Friedrich, it seemed. So he continued reluctantly, hoping the man would understand. "We are held in employment by the Count you see. We struck a bargain with him. He needs people like us to run certain errands, bring him certain supplies that he cannot otherwise arrange himself because … well, you have probably worked out why. So he spares us from becoming one of his victims so long as we run his errands and pass on to him stray travellers. We pretend the inn is full and that the Count has accommodation on his land that they can use. We send word to the Count and his horseman picks up the travellers. We have lived in peace that way for many years now."

Frederich added helplessly, "You had said that you were travelling through as part of your botany research, and that no one back home new exactly where you were, so you were a prime candidate you see for passing onto the Count. No one could trace you here and no one would miss you.

"But no one has ever escaped before! Did you fight off the horseman? How did you manage to escape the Count?"

Finally, the stranger gave him a faint smile, and looked out towards the window. The innkeeper followed his gaze apprehensively. This was not a friendly smile. The storm was dying down, and it was finally possible to see the sky. It was almost evening. Friedrich's stomach lurched towards his throat as the realisation drew on him. He glanced to the floor and it confirmed his fears: the man had left no trace of snow or wet footprints. He swallowed hard. The storm had blocked the sunlight, and that's how the man had been able to walk to the inn. He had made the mistake of inviting the man into the inn as an act of guilty hospitality, the man could only enter the premises once invited. And now here he sat opposite what was now more ghoul than man. Friedrich slowly looked up at his guest, hoping he was wrong, realising that there was no escape if he wasn't.

He saw the man's mouth widen to a full smile.

ETERNAL MAGIC

THE MAID POURED more wine into the glasses. She looked nervously at the woman at the head of the table. How would the master treat this one? His new wife was so much younger than him, and hardly spoke. He probably found her malleable, just the kind he liked. She had heard him refer to his new wife as 'The Mouse' to his lascivious friends, old men who saw women as property, and who congratulated him on his latest acquisition.

The master had had a string of wives, more than the King of England, but in his case none were beheaded. He either divorced them or they died of 'natural causes'. She didn't hold out much hope for this one, as handsome as she was, her looks would not save her. The maid had never heard her speak, that probably suited her master, but she wondered if she was mute. And that black ribbon that she always wore around her neck regardless of the dress she was wearing. The maid dwelled briefly on how it would be removed tonight. Her master enjoyed asserting his authority with a squeeze of the neck.

"Prepare my lady's room," he instructed. The maid gave a short curtsey and repaired upstairs, her stomach in knots as she remembered the first night for the previous wives. How would tonight end? She was scarred by the screams of torture from the previous wives.

He waited until they were alone, and then raised a toast

to his new wife. She sat silent and didn't appear to have eaten anything, merely playing with the food. "Agnes, my dear," he said in his best warm tone, "We are alone at last! It has been a long day. I see that the excitement has left you lacking an appetite. Perhaps we should retire now. I will show you to your room and join you presently."

She nodded in assent at his suggestion. He downed his wine and walked over to her and offered her his arm. He always behaved the impeccable gentleman in public. She took his arm and he led her up the stairs to where her bed chamber was located. He couldn't wait for her to be relieved of all her garments, heavy silks, linen underlayers and corsets. They were just obstacles to his final objective.

He stopped outside her chamber. "This is your room. Joan will have lit a fire and will help you undress. I will come to you in a short while." She gave him a steely look, which unnerved him slightly. Normally she looked slightly afraid of him, which is how he liked to be viewed. This new gesture of assertiveness was disconcerting, but he reminded himself that soon he would make his mark as her master.

He went to his room and drank a few glasses of whisky. He loved the anticipation of the excitement to come. He hummed happily to himself as he prepare to consummate yet another marriage.

He took a candle and walked along the corridor to her chamber. When he opened the door, he was struck by the darkness. There was no fire lit. no candles burning, and the room felt icy. His eyes adjusted to the silhouettes in the room and he saw his wife leaning out of the window in her nightdress, staring at the moon.

"Agnes! What do you think you are doing? Get back here at once! Someone might see you exposed like that!" He shouted at her angrily.

Agnes turned around slowly, and smiled at him, her hair falling loose around her. The moonlight made her dress transparent. He caught his breath, his fury intensifying his excitement.

"Have you no shame? Shut the window and come here at once!"

Agnes just laughed and walked over slowly to him. Such impertinence! What was she playing at? He placed the candle on the dressing table and as soon as she was within reach, he grabbed her neck and squeezed tightly.

"Don't you ever behave like a slut again!" he spat at her. She laughed again, seemingly unaffected by him half strangling her. Then she stopped and looked at him determinedly. "I will behave as I want, *Master.*" The last word was uttered in sarcasm.

He shook her. "I will teach you a thing or two about obedience!" he threatened, and with that, he tore off the black ribbon around her neck with one hand and ripped at the nightdress in fury with the other. The candle illuminated her body in yellow glow, highlighting ... everything ...

He stumbled backwards in shock. "What is the meaning of this? What trickery have you played on me?" He didn't want to look at her body. Her once smooth, creamy skin was now covered in angry welts, patches of burnt skin, and other scars the origins of which he didn't want to deduce.

"I have played no tricks on you, Master" That sarcasm again. "Do you not remember me?"

He shook his head. "Who are you? What sorcery have you performed? You never had those marks before!"

She walked towards him slowly. "Does this not give you a clue?" She pointed to the scar on her neck. The rings of red from a noose dug into the skin. That is what she had been covering with her black ribbon.

The only women he knew who had hanged were …

"Oh no!" he cried in shock. "It can't be!"

"Oh yes!" She smiled at him, arms outstretched, ready to embrace him. "It can be. Many years ago, I refused your advances. You had me condemned as a moon witch, sent to prison and tortured. You came to visit and claimed me regardless. You thought that my execution would kill the magic. But you see, the body may die, but the soul and the magic are eternal. You were desperate to have me, and I have returned to you. Now we can be together forever."

The maid stood cautiously outside the chamber door after a respectable time, but instead of screams from the lady, she heard triumphant laughter.

MARCH

DEATH MOON

SÉANCE OF THE DAMNED

THE MAID USHERED in another gentleman who looked the epitome of respectable in his tween suit and red cravat, whilst sporting a finely groomed moustache.

"Mr Pilkington!" exclaimed a delighted Madam Esher. She liked the title *Madam* as she felt it added to the sense of occasion. In fact she was just Mrs Esher, widowed. "I'm so glad you could join us," she smiled, clasping her hands.

"Well, you know how I feel about these things," responded Mr Pilkington.

"Indeed, sir, but we must not give up hope of making contact with the other side," said Madam Esher soothingly in her best hostess tone of voice. She smoothed the folds of her silk dress which shone in hues of dark green and purple in the gas light, suggesting a certain amount of wealth, and adding to the crackling atmosphere of anticipation.

She led Mr Pilkington to the parlour where there were another man and two women seated around a table. The younger woman blushed at seeing Mr Pilkington's wiry frame enter the room. Mr Pilkington gave a slight bow and addressed the company formally: "Sir Davenport, Lady Davenport …" He paused and said more tenderly, "Miss Francombe, it is always a pleasure to see you." The young lady bowed her head in coy embarrassment.

"We're glad you could join us, my good fellow!" roared Lord Davenport happily and got up to shake Mr Pilkington's hand. "Elspeth here gets very nervous about these events, don't you dear?" He beamed at the young lady. "It always helps having you here with her," he added with a chuckle and a wink and slapping Mr Pilkington's back. Mr Pilkington was too refined to respond to such jibes.

Madam Esher indicated to Mr Pilkington to take the vacant seat next to Elspeth. Mr Pilkington obliged, but not without a deep intake of breath, signifying his reluctance at the evening's proceedings.

"Well, now we're all here, let us all commence. I feel the souls gathering on the other side," said Madam Esher theatrically. She turned to the maid and said, "Elizabeth, dim the lights, we are about to proceed." The gaslights were duly dimmed so that the candelabra at the centre of the table could illuminate the apprehension on the faces around the table.

Madam Esher took her seat. "We must link hands," she instructed. "Remember, we must not break the circle. If the circle is broken, our different realms could collide."

Most of the guests held adjacent hands tentatively. Mr Pilkington sighed at what he perceived to the theatrics, but tentatively took the hands of Elspeth and Madam Esher. Now the theatrics truly began. Madam Esher took deep breaths and lowered her voice an octave.

"Spirits!" she cried. "Spirits! We are here! Can you hear us …?" She shook her head. "They are not ready yet. We must wait." There was a note of frustration in her voice. The grandfather clock clicked rhythmically in the background.

Everyone felt impatient. Madam Esher felt Mr Pilkington try to remove his hand from her grasp and impulsively tightened her grip. "No, Mr Pilkington!" she said firmly. "We must not break the circle. We must be ready when they come to us."

Lord Davenport stared at Mr Pilkington angrily. Mr Pilkington acquiesced but not without protest. "We could have had a quick drink in this time," he muttered in annoyance. Elspeth stifled a giggle, the others glared. Suddenly, Madam Esher bolted forward, her bosom heaving heavily with exertion. "I sense them!" she cried excitedly. "I can feel them trying to make contact with us! Spirits! Oh Spirits! I hear you! We are here!"

"Ask them if Tommy is there!" said Lady Davenport with urgency.

"Spirits!" Madam Esher continued in her best bass tone. "Is there a man called Tommy with you …? No, not Tony, TOMMY!"

"Oh for Goodness Sake!" cried Lord Davenport, angrily slamming his fists against the table and alarming his wife and Elspeth who sat either side of him and with whom his hands were linked.

The table shuddered at his violence.

"Lord Davenport! Control yourself!" Madam Esher admonished him.

"They always get it wrong!" said Lord Davenport angrily. "They come up with Tony, Tori, Terry, but never TOMMY!"

"Our realms do not have channels for clear communication. We can only sense what our guide is thinking," explained Madam Esher patiently.

Then she shut her eyes, breathed heavily and said, "No,

Spirits! We are still here. We are asking for Tommy. No, there is no one called Edith with us. Elspeth? Yes! We do have an Elspeth!"

Everyone looked at Elspeth in excitement. At last, a positive outcome! Elspeth looked in shocked and returned their gaze open mouthed.

"Oh my dear Elspeth, it is your sister Anne! She wants you to know that she misses you, and that your mother regrets the stern words she said." Madam Esher smiled at Elspeth triumphantly, finally feeling validated at her gift with communicating with the other side.

Elspeth remained open mouthed, and finally recovering her senses, she said timidly, "But I don't have any sister called Anne."

Groans circulated the table.

"Well I may have got the name wrong dear, the channels of communication aren't clear as I've explained. What was the name of your sister, dear?" asked Madam Esher.

Elspeth looked frightened., but plucking up her courage, she said, "I never had a sister!"

There were exclamations all around and Mr Pilkington could refrain his fury no longer. He pulled his hands sharply out of the grips of Madam Esher and Elspeth, startling both ladies, and knocked the table as he stood up and caused the candles to tremble.

"Madam Esher! I have had enough of your parlour tricks! You are nothing but a charlatan! Can't you see you're distressing everyone with your games? Lady Davenport will not meet her son Tommy until he dies. Elspeth will not be reunited with her family until they too die. Elspeth and I will never be married now as I had longed for. This is our reality! This is what we must face up to!" And with that impassioned speech, he slammed his fists on the table in anger just as Lord Davenport had done, and stormed out. The remaining company stared after him, mouths agape. Madam Esher clutched her corset in distress and rang for her maid to bring her a glass of brandy. Lord Davenport could be heard cursing Mr Pilkington's impudence whilst Lady Davenport sobbed uncontrollably.

MEANWHILE, IN THE land of the living, another party had gathered around a table with hands linked. At the head sat a lady with an over made face, black shawl and red haired wig for added effect. "My spirit guide is present. She is asking for someone. Someone whose name begins with 'T' … Tony! The name is Tony! Does anyone here know a Tony?" Everyone looked at each other nervously, when suddenly, *THUD!* As if someone had hit the table, making a sharp noise and causing the candles to shake. There were excited whispers all around. There was a spirit with them! But no one knew a Tony … at least, not a deceased one …

BACK IN THE realm of the dead, Elspeth, looked vacantly at the space left behind by Mr Pilkington. Why had he not made his intentions clear when they were alive? A tear ran slowly down her cheek. It was the first time Mr Pilkington had spoken of his intention to marry her. All this time she had thought he just took pity on her, showering her with attention when no one else had. Now they were stuck in the spirt world, trapped in a purgatory of unhappiness through unresolved issues from when they were alive. But tonight she felt contentment. Oblivious to the histrionics of Madam Esher, and the rage and upset of Lord and Lady Davenport, she slowly dissolved away from the realm with a smile.

THE CONFESSION

"LEAVE MY WIFE out of this!"

Passers-by looked at me sharply, but I didn't care what they thought, another drunk in the park. I took another swig from my can of beer.

The woman next to me smiled knowingly. "Well you know what you need to do if you want me to stay silent."

I continued to avoid her gaze. "She doesn't need to know. This is between you and me."

The woman laughed without mirth. "What are you afraid of? That she will leave you? You are at fault here, you deserve everything that's coming to you."

I took a sideway glance at her profile, flinched in anticipation, and then relaxed. Just a plain looking woman, the kind that would be invisible in a crowd with nothing to suggest that she had a malicious streak. I wished our paths had never crossed. I had been weak.

"You destroyed my life, now I want to destroy yours." I look down with anger and remorse bubbling up inside me. "Don't you think I can't stop thinking about you? Don't you think I wish with all my heart I could turn back the clock? Look, this isn't my wife's fault, this is all my doing. You don't need to speak to her." More beer. Just numb the pain, that's all I needed the beer to do. If I passed out it would be a bonus.

"That's the most honourable thing you've said so far," she

said with a hint of sarcasm. "But it doesn't change things. You need to pay for your actions, and I won't leave you until you do."

I crushed the beer can in silent anger and plucked another one out of the carrier bag at my feet.

"Have a heart! I have kids. They're still young, they need their father. I can't leave them. I won't leave them." I just about held back the tears, overwhelmed by a rush of love for them.

"What about my kids? Did you think about them? Did you think about the impact to my family? You are just too selfish to think about anyone but yourself!"

Her words cut through me like a razor blade. "Shut up, you evil whore!" I shouted. More shocked looks from the people around me, more whispering and giggling.

She laughed in pleasure at my pain. "Ironic statement coming from you. You want me to leave you, you know what to do." I sensed that she had turned to look at me directly. "Look at me," she said softly. I looked the other way. "I SAID, LOOK AT ME!" She repeated, her voice brimming with hate and determination.

I took another gulp of beer, it would give me courage, and slowly turned to look at her.

One half of her face looked normal. Just that plain woman, could be a teacher, a librarian, a job that didn't need ambition. The other half of her face was inhuman with flesh hanging loose off the cheeks, eyeball swinging out of the socket, the rest just a mass of blood and bruising. I had done this to her. I had been out drinking late one night. Just one drink, I had promised myself, but I always was useless with promises. Then I had to go home in time for an important meeting the next day. I thought the roads would be empty that late at night – who walks on unlit country roads in those early hours? How did I know she would be running out to find her dog? I didn't see her. I felt the bump, I saw a shadow cross my field of vision, but I just kept driving … and driving … and trying to ignore the possibility. I read about the hit and run a few days later. I kept trying to ignore it. But she came back to me, and she wasn't going to leave me.

The fight suddenly sank out of me.

"A life for a life." She stared at me like a cross-eyed monster.

"A life for a life," I repeated after her. I picked up my bag and started the slow walk home. "You already have my life, I have no life since the accident. I am a shadow of the man I was. Is that not enough?"

That mirthless laughter became a diminuendo as I walked away.

APRIL

PINK MOON

MONSTER DATE

COURTNEY SAUNTERED ONTO the stage excitedly. She loved fame, she had always wanted to be famous. This wasn't reality TV show kind of fame, as this was just a local social club rather than a TV show, but to be recognised locally would be a start! Who knew what avenues it would open. She would have totally missed the call for contestants had it not been for some new friends she had made when out clubbing. They were more sophisticated than her usual circle of friends, they made her feel special and grown up, even if she was in her early 20s. They had told her she was perfect for this 'Blind Date' event taking place at the social club. It sounded fun. It was in the same format as the TV show on which it was based: Courtney would sit on one side of a screen with three men whom she hadn't met or seen on the other side. Courtney would ask three questions and the men would give their responses, based on which Courtney would pick one of the men to go on a date with.

The spotlight shone on the host, a tall lady with jet black hair and wearing a heavily sequinned black dress. She looked deathly pale, but perhaps that was from the lights, thought Courtney.

There was a huge cheer and clapping from the crowd which Courtney relished. She tried to seek out her friends in the crowded room but it was too dark to make out any figures.

The host led Courtney to the chair on her side of the screen. "Welcome Courtney! I am Valentyna, your host for tonight."

Courtney sat down, hoping her white skirt suit was not too revealing. She felt very exposed on the stage.

"We all know the rules of the game, so let's begin!" said Valentyna excitedly. There was some laughter from the crowd and then hushing noises. "Well, Courtney, having seen the men on the other side of the screen, I can tell you now that you are in for a treat! We have three very special men on the other side."

"I'm so excited to be here!" exclaimed Courtney. "I can't wait to meet them!"

"And I'm sure they can't wait to eat you ..." There was a lot of sniggering again in the audience.

"Huh?" Courtney was puzzled.

"I said that the men couldn't wait to meet you."

"Oh!" said Courtney, relieved.

"What is your first question, Courtney?" Valentyna's voice was like treacle.

"Um ..." Courtney consulted the cards she held in her hands. "Well, I love a good night out. Where would you take me for a romantic night out?"

"Contestant number 1," said Valentyna, "Where would you take Courtney for a romantic night out?"

"I would take Courtney out for a romantic boat ride on the river, followed by a moonlit walk through the woods where I would display my animal magnetism, and really get the party going!" said a gruff voice that slowly escalated into excitement. There were approving noises from the audience.

"And contestant number 2?" asked Valentyna.

"I would take Courtney out for a romantic candlelit meal, followed by some intimate dancing where I would show her my best moves, cheek to cheek, neck to neck, and my effusive charm would be enough to make her blood tingle." The audience laughed. Courtney didn't understand what was so funny, so laughed along too, a little nervously.

"And Contestant number 3 ..."

There was a grunt in a response, then silence. Courtney looked up to Valentyna. "I'm sorry, I didn't catch what he said."

Valentyna smiled sweetly at Courtney without showing her teeth. "He says he would take you to a graveyard at night, as being the living amongst the dead would really make you feel alive! He would then do his impression of Michael Jackson's thriller routine to really set the mood."

Courtney frowned, but then smiled politely at Valentyna and giggled nervously again as the audience broke into an uproarious roar.

"And what is your second question?"

Courtney read from her card again. "Food is one of my greatest pleasures in life, and I love to try new restaurants with great ambience. Where would you take me for a romantic meal out that's a little bit different to the norm?"

"Contestant number 1?"

"I appreciate the quality of food, so I would take you somewhere where the meat is at its freshest and reared properly. We would go to a cabin in the woods and eat under the light of a full moon ..." said the first man. "Accompanied by full blooded wine," he added, apparently much to the audience's delight. Blooded wine? Thought Courtney, confused. Maybe he had said full bodied wine and she had misheard.

"Contestant number 2?"

"I would take Courtney for a meal in a castle, away from prying eyes, where we can enjoy the best quality food and finest wine against the warmth of a log fire and the splendour of wealth. We could be King and Queen for a night." This response elicited a lot of 'Ooooohs' from the audience. Courtney nodded her head in approval.

"And lastly, contestant number 3."

There was another grunt.

"I'm finding it hard to understand him," Courtney whispered to Valentyna.

"He says he would take you for a meal in a mausoleum, where you will be waited on by spirited people and be surrounded by a magical atmosphere."

"Oh ..." Courtney looked a little startled at this response. Number 3 wasn't what she was expecting from any of the contestants.

"And your final question?"

Courtney adjusted herself in her seat for the final question and paused for dramatic effect. "I love trying out new cocktails. If you could invent a cocktail for me, what kind of cocktail would it be and why?"

"Great last question! Number 1, what kind of cocktail would you create?"

"My cocktail for you would be both strong and spicy with a hint of sweetness, to reflect my strength and your sweet nature. It would be strong enough to put hairs on your chest." The audience erupted in laughter. Courtney grinned, her nerves finally giving way to enjoyment.

"And Number 2 ..." said Valentyna as the laughter died down.

"My cocktail for you would be vibrant and blood red, to showcase how full of life you are. When you drink my cocktail, it will make your teeth itch for more and you will feel my power ..." he said dramatically. The audience laughed hysterically, but Courtney frowned, confused by part of his response.

"Did he just say I would feel his power?" she asked Valentyna in a low voice.

"No," Valentyna whispered back, "he said you would feel *more* power."

"Oh," said Courtney simply, but she was still confused by the response.

"And lastly, number 3."

A similar grunt was emitted from the other side of the screen.

Courtney shook her head at Valentyna. "I still don't get what he says," she admitted.

"He said his cocktail would be so powerful it could raise the dead, because he can tell without meeting you just how powerful you are ..." The audience started guffawing again. Courtney seemed happy with the response.

"So Miss Courtney, have you decided which one you would like to go on a date with?" Valentyna looked at her expectantly.

Courtney squirmed in her seat with delight and lied, "Well I loved all the answers, but there's no doubt in my mind who gave the best responses. I choose" – another dramatic pause for effect – "Number 3!"

Valentyna gasped in surprise, the audience gasped in surprised, much whispering could be heard. "Number 3? Are you sure?" asked Valentyna, still dumbfounded.

"Oh yes, absolutely certain!" cried Courtney with new-found confidence.

Valentyna nodded her head in acknowledgement and got Courtney to stand up. "Then let us see who you disappointed tonight! Number 1, can you please walk around and reveal yourself!"

Courtney squealed in delight as she saw a tall man emerge from behind the screen. He was very handsome, but had an abundance of bodily hair which made her tingle and scratch all over as they embraced. She felt a slight scratch on her neck and felt him being pushed back by Valentyna who was muttering under her breath, "Don't even think about it if you don't want to be paid in silver!"

Courtney didn't know what this meant but she mouthed an apology the man sulked off the stage. The audience clapped and whooped excitedly.

"Number 2, please come around and reveal yourself!" A tall, dark, but not quite handsome man came out to greet Courtney. He looked deathly pale and when he smiled, he looked as if he required dental surgery. His eyes were hypnotic, and she didn't want to embrace him but his arms were wrapped around her before she knew it, squeezing her tightly and she again felt a scratch on her neck. Valentyna was quick to the rescue once more. "Keep off her unless you want stake for dinner!" Courtney didn't understand the threat but was grateful for Valentyna's intervention.

Finally! The big reveal!

"Are you ready to see Number 3, your blind date for this evening?" asked Valentyna.

"I am a bit nervous now," giggled Courtney excitedly, and the audience giggled with her.

"We will now pull back the screen and reveal your blind date!"

Someone behind the curtains worked a mechanical device to reveal contestant number 3. The audience held their breath, Valentyna smiled sweetly again at Courtney.

As the last of the screen tugged away, Courtney stood in shock as she saw a tall man, skin decaying, covered in lesions and hanging loose off his face, arms outstretched presumably for an embrace. The audience cheered in delight as they watched Courtney cover her mouth and scream through her hands. Finally she would realise that she had been picking supernatural beings for her date. But Courtney did something that stopped them in their tracks. She screamed but not in fear as they had assumed, but in delight! She then hugged the zombie enthusiastically, kissing both his pustule ridden cheeks. The zombie had never felt an emotion, but he was also startled by this turn of events.

Courtney jumped up and down with joy and turned to Valentyna who was uncharacteristically stunned into silence.

"I can't believe it!" she cried happily. "He's my perfect date. Wait till Mum and Dad hear about this. I was raised to eat human flesh you see, but it's damned near impossible to find a date who shares my taste for dead humans. But I have finally found my perfect match!" And with that, she clasped the zombie's hands and kissed him again affectionately. The zombie felt something within him other than hunger, and smiled back at her.

KITCHEN GOD

PENG WATCHED WITH his usual fascination as his mother dusted the shrine in the kitchen, a small corner devoted to the Kitchen Deity, a picture of whom was hung on a scroll on the wall and in front of which lay accoutrements of worship. His mother offered a chant to the picture and lit the candles and incense, and placed small cakes in a brass bowl as offerings to the Kitchen God.

Peng sub-consciously licked his lips – these happened to be one of his most favourite cakes. They were expensive and only bought for special occasions. It seemed the Kitchen God had graced his mother with eyes at the back of her head and mind reading skills when it came to Peng's plans for secret raids in the kitchen. His seven year old mind rarely succeeded in outwitting his mother. He wondered if there was a gambling God too for his mother's other great passion. She had never mentioned one and he knew better than to ask.

His mother seemed to sense his eyes on the cakes and turned to look at him sharply. "Don't try to steal the cakes from the Kitchen God or he will be sure to punish you!" She looked at him sternly for a few seconds to let the threat sink in.

"Yes, Mother," responded Peng in his most obedient tone, wondering what event had led his mother to offer up such expensive cakes.

That night, when the family had all retired for the evening, Peng snuck across to the kitchen. Surely neither the Kitchen God nor his Mother would know if just one small cake went missing? His stomach growled in anticipation of the culinary delight to come.

The moon shone through the window and illuminated the picture of the Kitchen God. Peng crept up to the shrine. There was something about the picture that unnerved him. No matter where he stood in the kitchen, the Kitchen God's eyes seemed to follow him, The Kitchen God wore a smile that could best be described as malevolent.

Peng raised one small hand up towards the brass bowl full of the cakes. In an instant one of the candles lit up by itself! Peng gasped and pulled back his hand in amazement and fear. How did it light by itself? And then he frowned … the Kitchen God's smile now looked mocking, as if Peng had dared to try to out-do the Kitchen God. Peng felt determination rise within him. He gave the Kitchen God a menacing stare, clenched his fists, and quickly made for the cakes before the Kitchen God could take any action. But the Kitchen God was too quick for Peng: the lit candle fell over and hot wax dripped onto Peng's hand. Peng let out a scream and as he pulled back his hand in agony and knocked the brass bowl over the counter and smash onto the tiled floor with an immense *CLANG!*

Suddenly, the whole kitchen was lit up as the shadow of his mother loomed across the floor tiles like a demon coming to claim its prey. He heard her scream, 'PENG!'

Her fury made his little body shake in horror of his mother's presence. He looked up at the Kitchen God, who looked back at him with a victorious smile. He had been defeated once again by the Kitchen God ...

LEERIE

"LEERIE … OH LEERIE …!"

When Dougal first heard the wind whisper the Scottish nickname for his trade, he thought it was someone trying to get his attention. He hollered back, he looked around, but there was no one there.

Leerie.

The slang for Lamplighter.

Well, part illuminator of the streets, part night watchman. Every night without fail, he would walk the streets with his ladder, supply of oil, spare wicks, and a long pole with a wick to light the street oil lamps. He replaced wicks and topped up the oil as required. Then he would return just before sunrise, the wick on his pole replaced by a hook, to extinguish the lights.

He would walk for miles in this way, and worked for a pittance. It seemed fitting that he should repair shoes to supplement his income, as he was forever wearing through his boots.

He was taught this trade by a miserable old man who very reluctantly explained the simple procedures to him. The man went through every procedure, and before they parted, he said. 'Beware of the mist. Stay out of their way." Dougal had said nothing, thinking that maybe that is why the light company was getting rid of this lamplighter, it was obvious this man was going senile. The old man gave him a pitying look, shook his head in despair and walked off, leaving Dougal standing with the pole and ladder to do his first shift alone.

Dougal was full of energy when he first started the job, but the spring in his step was reduced to a weary trudge after months of little sleep and the laborious walking, trying to ignite and extinguish the lamps on time.

He paid no heed to the shadows at first. It was only when the haar, the cold, sea mist, rolled into Edinburgh, that he first noticed he wasn't alone. It was the kind of night when people were most grateful for the gas lights that afforded a few metres of illumination against the forbidding blanket of grey that had descended on the city. He was descending a ladder after replacing a wick, and focussing on the ground to keep himself steady, when he noticed a shadow of a man standing by the ladder. There was no solid form to accompany the shadow.

When he reached the ground he looked around and spoke to the empty air, asking if anyone was there. And that's when he heard that beckoning voice within the haar:

"Leerie … Oh Leerie …!"

He hollered loudly, but no one responded. And yet the shadow stood, waiting. A trick of the light, thought Dougal, one's imagination can run riot on nights like this. And so he walked on to the next lamp, but the shadow followed, a little to his side, and a little behind him. His own shadow was distinctive as he carried the pole and ladder, but this shadow seemed to be of an empty handed man. It followed Dougal until the last lamp. It followed Dougal when he returned to extinguish the lights. It stopped when Dougal stopped, it moved as Dougal moved.

Dougal wasn't scared of the shadow at first, more intrigued. He actually came to see it as a companion on a lonely night, and started talking to it. Thankfully there weren't many people around on such an evening. Even if they did hear him, the fog was so thick they assumed he was talking to someone out of their line of sight.

He didn't see the shadow again until the city was enveloped in the thick sea fog again. The shadow reappeared. It followed him like last time. But the shadows had become bolder, more of them emerged. He saw the silhouettes of ladies with bags or umbrellas walk past him as he tended the lamps, while his male shadow companion stood silently waiting for him. He saw silhouettes of gentlemen wearing fine hats come from the other direction, raising their arm as if to tip their hat to acknowledge him. He touched his cap in silent acknowledgement.

It was after a year that he saw the other side of the shadows, and came to understand there were not harmless outlines of poor souls. If he took too long to tend to a lamp, several shadows gathered around him, and he could sense them waiting impatiently as he finally lit the lamp. They did not break the circle to let him pass, so he had to walk over the shadows. He felt his blood turn to ice. Any congeniality that had existed between him and the shadows evaporated. Apparently they were expecting him to perform a service for them.

It was a few months later that he discovered their true intent. They only appeared when the sea cast its mist on the land, but on this occasion he noticed a shadow follow a young man. He could only watch for the small area of ground that was visible, but he saw the man stop abruptly as if suddenly paralysed. A black cloud formed around the man's feet and spread up his body, and then the cloud dispersed and both man and shadow were gone.

Dougal stood rooted to the spot, numb with shock. He never drank on duty, and he didn't doubt what he had witnessed. Now the shadows had taken on a different complexion, they had gone from being the mysterious unwanted presence to some evil entity that could harm the living.

Shadows crowded around him again, he felt their threatening presence. They wanted him to carry on lighting the lamps. He became fearful now. He needed the money, he couldn't afford to walk away from this job. He felt afraid and trapped. Now he understood the old man who had taught him the trade. If he ignored them and stuck diligently to his job, he would come to no harm. He couldn't warn other people as the shadows could easily claim him. They would mock him through the haar by calling out to him, "Leerie … Oh Leerie …!" But he ignored the whisper in his ear.

He resolved to find the previous Leerie to find out who they were. A few enquiries led him to a tavern tucked away in a narrow street.

"You've seen them then," It was more a statement than a question. "They are the folk who drowned at sea. The sea mist transports their souls from sea to land. They seem bitter about losing their life, and want to walk the streets like they used to rather than rot in the watery grave, but they can only stay as long as the mist lasts, and they need the lamps lit so they can see the street. The really angry ones will take a life out of spitefulness at their own purgatory. They follow you to make sure you light the lamps. Do not engage with them, for if you do anything that brings them displeasure, well, you know the rest …"

MAY

FLOWER MOON

GHOST MARRIAGE

THEY MET ON a spring evening beneath the cherry blossom, delicate petals of pink fluttering around them like confetti, as if they were already at their wedding day. Indeed, both were dressed in their finest clothes.

"You are very pretty. My parents have chosen well." He addressed her like a delicate flower.

She blushed in return and looked down as was expected of her after such a compliment. She had not had time to take in all his features. She couldn't say he was handsome, just plain looking, but respectable. She didn't think his dark rimmed glasses suited him, they made him look geeky.

"It is an honour to finally meet you. My parents have also chosen well." She returned the compliment in a reverent tone, and bowed her head further as a gesture of respect and acceptance. She looked up slowly. He was smiling, displaying his crooked teeth that resembled tortilla crisps in a cavernous mouth. She suppressed a gasp of disappointment. What had her parents seen in him?

At first she had been excited to be paired with a man, any man, but now she felt revulsion.

"It will be so nice to have a companion at last," he said pleasantly, oblivious to her disappointment. She swallowed hard and forced a smile.

"Yes!" she agreed, "No more solitary days!" She bit her nails nervously. He did not like that in a woman, all that fidgeting, so undignified, he would have to correct her manners after they were married. But he would allow her to fidget for the moment.

"My parents told me you studied art," he tried to continue the conversation.

"Yes," she suddenly brightened. "I wanted to specialise in the conservation of art, but then ..." She left the sentence hanging. She couldn't bring herself to remember that day. She didn't want to think about the conservation of her own body as a result. At least her dress was concealing the worst of it, and make up made her miraculously look normal. She examined him more closely. She couldn't see many scars on him. She was too scared to ask him that very personal question that was the forefront of her mind.

"My parents told me of your accident," he said gently. She felt relief wash over her. Then he changed tack. "Your degree is of no use now," he said pompously. She looked at him stunned. The degree was an important achievement in her life. It had given her status, a sense of accomplishment, a standing within her community.

"What did you study?" she asked whilst restraining herself from adding, *"If you studied at all."*

"I studied economics," he replied proudly. She should have guessed by his expensive suit. "I had the highest marks for all the modules in my year." And with that he rambled on about academic and professional achievements. "And what good is your Masters degree and your promotion here?" she asked scathingly. She could say such unbecoming things here. There were no special social norms to follow now there was no one to judge them.

He looked shocked. How dare she answer him back like that!

"Evidently my parents weren't warned about your sharp tongue!" he said bitterly.

"Nor mine about your hubris!" she retorted angrily. She saw his cheeks flush, fists clenched. She wondered if he would strike her, but they were not permitted to touch before the ceremony. Finally he drew a deep breath and gave a forced laugh. "Listen to us! We are not even married and we are having our first argument!"

She smiled in resignation. "Yes, let us call a truce. The ceremony is not too far away now." The longer she was with him, the more repulsive she found him. Both in body and mind. If he was so rich why couldn't he do something to improve his appearance? Probably women had flocked to him for his money. Thank goodness her friends would never meet him. They would tell her she was too good for him.

She finally picked up the courage to ask, "How did you come to be here?"

His face fell in shame. He could no longer meet her gaze. "I was murdered after accruing gambling debts I couldn't pay off. The more I earned, the more I lost on the tables."

She nodded, but without sympathy. Such showman that he was, he was a failure in part of his life, as most people are. "I should go," she said at last. She turned to leave but he stopped her.

"Wait! I just need you to know, I really am glad my parents chose you." She held his gaze but said nothing, she would not give an equal sentiment back. After a few moments she walked away feeling the hopelessness of the situation press on her heart, as if her spiritual body had become flesh again.

THE FOLLOWING EVENING, they stood side by side and watched the ceremony beneath the blossom tree. Their corpses had been dug up and the coffins placed side by side whilst a priest read the wedding vows. Their families sobbed with remorse, relief, and sorrow melded into one.

Their parents had been disturbed at the fact that their respective child had died unmarried and would have no one in the afterlife. They heard about the wedding ceremony for the deceased where corpses were wed and bound together in the spirit world.

The parents would visit the grave of their offspring and talk to them there, explaining the plan and reviewing potential partners. The newly bound couple looked on with a pervading sense of doom. They were now spiritually bound for eternity, their parents had unintentionally placed a prison sentence on them, where there was no chance of parole. There was no chance of divorce either. At the end of the ceremony, rice was thrown over the bodies to symbolise a spirit child they could never have. They glared at their coffins being lowered back into the earth, side by side. Without looking at each other, they walked away in opposite directions.

DOUBLE TAKE

THE MORNING WAS bright if a little chilly. This didn't deter Chloe from slipping into a Mary Quant rip-off mini dress and sandals. She was confident the sun wouldn't let her down today. Her friends would be coming over to see her new flat, a Victorian tenement with high ceilings, intricate cornices in the ceiling and creaking wooden floorboards, and a tiny back garden which was just big enough to host a barbeque. The flat was full of character, a sharp change from the prefab house her parents had decorated in tawny colours. Chloe was determined to decorate her flat in fresh, bright colours, a reflection of the excitement of using bold colours following the drabness of the post-war era.

Chloe made herself some toast and coffee and hummed happily as she traipsed over to the lounge which took full advantage of the sun through three large windows (no double glazing and extremely draughty, a repair which was beyond Chloe's budget at the moment). Chloe pushed open the lounge door and nearly dropped her coffee in shock.

Almost simultaneously, a woman in the lounge looked back at Chloe in equal shock.

"Who are you?" they both said at once.

The woman was able to compose herself as Chloe took in her appearance: she was dressed in a black silk gown with puffed sleeves, bodice, and white lace trimming, greying hair neatly tied into a bun. She folded her hands in front of her, straightened her back and said, "Young woman! What are you doing in my house! Why are you half naked? For God's sake girl, go and cover yourself up!"

Chloe's shock subsided into anger. "What am I doing in your house? What are you doing in MY house! And how dare you tell me how I should dress! You're the one dressed like a Victorian Granny!"

The woman gasped in shock and held a hand to her chest for dramatic effect. "Such impertinence! And to use the Good Queen's name in vain!"

Chloe was indignant. Was this someone's idea of a joke? "Did Rory send you? Is this a set up?" Chloe put down her toast and coffee on an unopened cardboard box, then placed her hands on her hips. "OK, I get the joke, I told friends this house is supposedly haunted and now one of my friends has put you up to this as a fun way of not disappointing me. You can stop the pretence now. Can I get you a coffee? Least I can do after all the effort you have made for me."

"Young lady, I have no idea about what you speak! As for ghosts, well … Oh … oh … oh!' A sudden realisation dawned on the woman and she sank back into an armchair that Chloe didn't recognise and could have sworn wasn't there when she had first gone into the room.

"Oh my!" gasped the woman. "A ghost! A real life ghost!"

Chloe was bemused. "Me? A ghost? You're the one dressed like a relic! You're the ghost, remember? Now which one of my friends put you up to this? They could have hired someone with a bit more intelligence than you."

"Young woman, I shall not be spoken to like that! Even if you are a ghost! Oh my!" She clutched at her breast again. "I need my smelling salts. Wait till I tell Myrtle about this, she will never believe I have seen a real ghost! Especially after all the seances she has held."

"Seances? Smelling salts?" Chloe almost laughed and walked over to where the woman sat, towering over her. "And Myrtle? Who calls anyone 'Myrtle' these days?" she said incredulously. "Aren't you taking this too far?"

The woman looked at her angrily. "I will show you which one of us is a ghost!" The woman picked up a small brass bell on a doily from a small table next to her.

Chloe was perplexed. Where did that table come from? And the bell? And a doily? Why would she have a doily in her house? That was the kind of adornment her mother liked around the house, but that was the kind of tired familiarity Chloe had escaped from.

The woman rang the bell. Small tinkles hung in the air despite the vigorous shake. They both heard heavy footsteps in the hallway. They looked at each other, Chloe confused, the woman clasped her hands and responded with a smug smile. Then they both frowned. It was a man's voice steadily getting louder as he approached the lounge.

"Yeah … Yeah … I'm just moving to another room, I haven't finished unpacking but I think the box with the brochures is there …"

The door swung open. There were three sharp intakes of breath. A man stood in the doorway, mouth agape, black wires coming out of his ears and holding a strange black rectangular item. The women frowned at him, also with mouths open. And then … Nothing!

"Oh my God!" said the man to the person on the

conference call. "You won't believe this, but I just saw two women here ... and ... and they just disappeared!"

There was a pause at the other end, and then laughter ... "Yeah right."

JUNE

ROSE MOON

THE KEENING

THE BOATMAN STOOD on the pier and studied the soldier trying to balance the duffle bag over his shoulder whilst steadying himself on a crutch. It was futile offering to help him.

It had been a rough crossing. You could tell a lot about a person's character through how they behaved during the crossing. The soldier had been unfazed, undoubtedly he had experienced worse when being shipped to the trenches in France.

The soldier and boatman locked eyes, the soldier seemed wary of the boatman but for no good reason.

"I leave at sunset. Be back by then," said the boatman, packing tobacco into his pipe and carefully sheltering it from the wind as he lit it, savouring the inhalations. It was going to be a long day.

"I'm not going back to the mainland, there is nothing left for me there," the soldier said flatly, and turned around to start his ascent up the path to his village.

"Theres nothing for you on this island either," retorted the boatman quietly once the soldier was out of earshot, and blew out perfect circles of smoke in weariness.

The soldier wondered if they would recognise him in the village. His posture had changed, he had grown into a man, he had allowed his stubble to grow after his discharge to try and cover up some of his facial scars. Beards and moustaches had been forbidden in the army as they made it difficult to wear a gas mask. It felt liberating to allow his facial hair to grow. He had dreamt of doing so many things once he left the army, but now he felt numb and empty, haunted by the sights, noises and stench of the trenches.

He was nervous of seeing his mother again. He had left silently one day because she had refused to let him sign up. His father had died when he was still a baby, so it had just been him and his mother all this time. She was scared of losing him too, but he had felt there was no future on the island. Now he had returned, and there was still no future for him, but for other reasons.

He climbed the hillock steadily, wincing at the effort. His leg throbbed and his hand bore the callouses of using the crutch for so long. The wind swirled around him, and he fancied he could hear it whistling in his ear. The whistling reminded him the sound of bullets. He stopped briefly as memories came flooding back, and again he pushed back his thoughts. He came here to forget, not remember.

Then he heard another sound in the wind, a low wailing noise that suddenly spiked in pitch, and then dipped again. It came closer and closer ... A keening! The islanders had maintained this traditional practice of lamenting for the dead during a funeral possession.

He scrambled as fast as his lame leg would allow to the top of the hillock and saw the steady stream of men and women in black below, a hearse in the middle. It was a couple of the elder women who were performing the keening. He didn't want to be disrespectful and disturb the procession as it made its way along the coffin path. So he waited until the procession had almost passed before he descended the hillock. Luckily the processions moved slowly because of the weight of the coffin, so he was able to catch up with the rear group of people. He recognised a few faces – everyone looked older than their years. He wondered what hardships they had suffered. Whatever they suffered, it was no match for the horrors he had felt. No one seemed to notice his presence behind them, which suited him. There was an older lady struggling to keep pace with everyone. Mrs Bannock! He would keep her company, her pace suited his limp.

He had grown up with Mrs Bannock telling him folk lore by the fireside, reading tea leaves for his mother, filling his mind with local superstitions.

He quickened his pace to stagger alongside her. She didn't seem to notice him at first, but then her head turned sharply towards him, she gasped in horror and covered her mouth to stifle a scream.

"Mrs Bannock! It's me, Archie!" He tried to reassure her. He knew that he had been away for a few years, he knew he bore a few scars, but he didn't think he looked that hideous.

Her small stout frame trembled next to him. "What are you doing here?" She hissed quietly so as not to arouse concern from others. "You shouldn't be here!"

He suddenly grew angry. "I have every right to be here! This is my home! I may have left without saying goodbye but I have every right to be here!"

"You don't understand …" Mrs Bannock shook her head in despair and tried to quicken her pace to get away from him.

"What don't I understand?" asked the soldier indignantly.

"Go back to the boat before it departs. There is nothing for you here." She spoke looking straight ahead, like he wasn't there at all.

"I've only just arrived! Of course I'm not going back!" he said indignantly. Then added, "Is my Mam here?"

"Don't you go near your Ma!" said Mrs Bannock angrily. "You made her suffer enough, you will make her even more distraught if she saw you now."

"What are you havering about, Mrs Bannock?"

Mrs Bannock glared at him. "Do you not understand whose funeral this is laddie? Do you not remember what I taught you about the boatman?"

The soldier stumbled on, confused, fragments of memory returning to him, trying to piece everything together. The boatman was like Charon of the River Styx, rowing people to the underworld. He allowed people a brief farewell on the island, and if they did not return to the boat in time, their spirit would be trapped until the next person on the island died, and only then could the spirit board the boat again.

A warm dampness spread across his chest. He looked down and saw a patch of red bloom out like a poppy through his uniform. The whistling of the artillery came back to him, explosions all around, and trying to protect his body. That is what Mrs. Bannock could see, not his illusion of wearing an intact uniform.

At least in death he couldn't feel pain. But the memories would still haunt him, he would always pervade fear and sadness around him. Could spirits be haunted by themselves?

"Go now! Before it's too late!" whispered Mrs Bannock urgently.

"I can't leave, not just yet, I need to say goodbye to Ma," he said tearfully.

"It will be too late!"

"I'm not leaving without saying goodbye to her."

"You will end up haunting her if you don't leave in time. Your spirt will become attached to her. Don't do this to her!"

Suddenly another voice interrupted them.

"Are you alright there, Mrs Bannock? Were you saying something?" a young lady was asking solicitously.

Mrs Bannock said gently, "No child, I was just mumbling some prayers aloud."

"I'll join you," said the young woman. "I understand you were very close to Archie when he was younger. You must miss him so much."

"It is better not to miss the dead too much, or they may remain with you," replied Mrs Bannock with a sidelong glance. The young lady frowned at this odd comment, but took Mrs Bannock's arm and started reciting a prayer to soothe the old lady.

Mrs Bannock turned to the soldier and mouthed with urgency, "GO!"

THE MAGIC CARPET

A BELL TINKLED playfully as Claire and David entered the shop. An antidote to all things minimalist, and yet more 'homely' than cluttered, it was an Aladdin's cave of Himalayan wares. At the front of the shop there was a range of Tibetan singing bowls, colourful papier-mâché desk accessories embellished with gold swirls, bohemian skirts and tops, and further back was a visual feast of autumnal and neutral coloured carpets with striking geometric patterns.

To the side, almost hidden by stacks of carpets, was an alcove. Intrigued, Claire and David entered it and felt they may have been transported to somewhere even more exotic. Inside there was a sofa and a couple of chairs covered in carpets, and on every wall hung more carpets. In the centre was a wooden coffee table with a detailed mother of pearl geometric floral design. It had the feel of a Bedouin tent with its textiles and natural furniture.

"You're welcome to sit inside," a young lady said to them. "Perhaps I could bring you some mint tea? We have a special Moroccan version with fresh mint and rose syrup. Or some Turkish coffee? We have only recently started serving hot drinks here, it adds to the ambience of the room," she smiled at them encouragingly.

"We would love that!" David said enthusiastically. "The tea sounds exotic, I will have that, please."

"And I'll have the tea as well, thanks," added Claire.

They took a seat on the sofa and absorbed their surroundings. The intricate designs of some of the carpets was to be admired. The carvings of the furniture was to be appreciated. Their drinks arrived in small glasses with delicate patterns and on glass saucers. On a teaspoon to the side of each class was a small delicate piece of rose shortbread.

"I could imagine Scheherazade dreaming up stories here," mused Claire, "One Thousand and One Nights, and so on." David took a sip of his coffee with great satisfaction at the aroma and intense taste. He leaned back and said dreamily, "Tell me a story then …"

"I can tell you a story …"

Claire and David sat bolt upright. They hadn't even noticed that someone had joined them in the alcove and was sitting on one of the chairs. How had that happened? They must have been too absorbed to notice him enter. He was a slim, dark middle-aged man in a cream suit, red kerchief and an immaculately trimmed pencil thin moustache. He could have been from another era, as if he had stepped out of an Agatha Christie story.

"I can tell you a story," he repeated, "about the carpet above you."

Claire and David swivelled around to look at the carpet above the sofa. It was as if fire had been captured on a rug, with its spiking patterns of hues of reds, oranges and yellows. They turned back to look at the man quizzically.

"What's so special about the carpet?" Asked Claire.

"It was possessed by a djinn," said the man, rhythmically stirring a small glass of tea which must have been served whilst they were distracted by the carpet.

"Gin?" asked David incredulously. "I become possessed by gins at the distillery next door!"

The man arched an eyebrow disapprovingly.

Claire glared at David whilst assuring the man, "Ignore him. We would love to know the story behind the carpet."

"Very well, I shall tell you." His quiet voice was laced with a Middle Eastern accent.

"Hundreds of years ago, a wealthy merchant was blessed by one daughter and no sons. So precious was the daughter, Alya, to him, that he paid a magician to have a djinn cast into a special carpet so that she could call upon the djinn for help in times of trouble. That is djinn as in genie, not the alcoholic drink." He looked pointedly at David, and continued, "The magician used his skills to turn a magical fire into a carpet, and then he cast a djinn into the carpet. In time Alya was married to someone who seemed to be genial and honourable, but he turned out to be volatile.

"Alya kept the carpet in the ladies' quarters, for men and women had separate living arrangements in those days, and the husband rarely entered the women's area. Alya summoned the djinn whenever she needed help, and he would appear as a servant so as not to arouse suspicion.

"In time though, the husband noticed how close his wife was to this servant and had him spied upon. When he was informed that the servant was in fact a djinn, for the spies had witnessed him disappearing into the carpet, the husband encouraged his wife to spend a few days away with friends and in her absence had the carpet removed. He asked a magician to exorcise the carpet and remove the djinn.

"However, the djinn was more powerful than the magician

and he overpowered and killed the magician. Then he took the form of the magician and when the husband returned, he convinced him that the exorcism had been successful and accepted a payment of a bag of gold. The husband was full of pride at outwitting his wife. The djinn encouraged him to talk. He pretended to join in the husband's disdain for women and the burden they were on men while making them both some tea, as was custom in those parts. People didn't drink alcohol in that part of the world, tea was the choice of drink for men. Men bonded over tea, deals were done over tea, social events centred around sitting on carpets and drinking tea. So the djinn brewed fresh mint tea, and added rose syrup to disguise the bitterness of the poison which he discreetly added to the husband's glass. He watched in satisfaction as the husband's laughter was cut short abruptly as the poison took effect.

"The djinn then rolled up the carpet, took the bag of money and returned to his Mistress. He had freed her both spiritually and financially from her husband. He served the next owners of the carpet after Alya had passed away, only revealing himself to those of a good disposition. But over time, people stopped believing in djinns and he was forgotten.

"If you look carefully at the carpet, you can see the signature of the djinn."

Claire and David turned around again on impulse to study the pattern. The colours seemed hypnotic, the pattern looked as if it might emerge out of the carpet and become a solid form.

Claire shook her head and said, "I don't see anything

..." She turned around to address the man but he had gone. "Where did he go?"

David had also turned back around. "He seems to appear and disappear out of nowhere!"

The young lady returned to check in on them. "Have you finished with your drinks?" she asked courteously.

"Not quite ..." said Claire. "Do you know where that man went?"

"Which man?"

"The man who was here with us. He was drinking tea with us and telling us a story, but then he just seemed to disappear.

The young woman smiled sympathetically at her. "You're the only ones I have served drinks to today. I can check with the other staff in case they have seen him?"

"No, that's quite alright. He must have left quietly."

"Well I'll leave you to finish your drinks in peace." The young woman left them alone.

Claire and David looked at each other with mild alarm, and then peered down into their respective glasses of half drunk rose and mint tea, but was that just the dredges of tea at the bottom of the glass?

They thought of the unsuspecting husband in the story, whose controlling nature had led the djinn to exact justice upon him through this beverage. A sense of surreal dread crept through them as each thought of their own weaknesses and insecurities which made them behave in an irrational manner at times. Did the djinn find their behaviour unacceptable? Had the djinn exacted justice for their perceived crimes through their mint tea?

They peered closer to the bottom of their glasses as they scoured for evidence of any substance that didn't look like tea ...

JULY

THUNDER MOON

COME TO ME

THE PHONE VIBRATED as if in anger, mirroring the emotions of the caller. His hands shook in unison with the phone as he clasped his shot of whisky. He dreaded to look at the caller display. He didn't want to talk to anyone, he wanted to wallow in his pain and self pity, let it suck him into an alcoholic black hole from which he wouldn't have to emerge. But how could he deny his only child? His daughter was cleaved to his heart, he felt like he could almost feel what she felt, hear her thoughts.

The phone stopped vibrating. He had long ago turned off the special ringtone he had for his family, the pain of hearing it was too much after they left him. His breathing became heavy, he could feel his daughter becoming angry, she would think he was ignoring her.

He had wanted to give his daughter everything he had been deprived of in his poverty stricken childhood. His wife would accuse him of spoiling her, but he thought her jealous of the special bond father and daughter had. The sacred family trinity that he had worked so hard to foster had been broken once his wife left him and took their daughter with her. He couldn't forgive his wife for that.

The phone started vibrating again, even more fiercely. He couldn't do this, couldn't break the ties with her. It was the mother he was angry with, not his daughter. He picked up the phone and answered the call but couldn't speak, his throat constricted with emotion. He was frightened. He didn't know what to say to her.

"Dad?" she sobbed. "I miss you, Dad. Why won't you come to see me?" There was silence at the other end of the phone, but she could hear the heavy breathing. "Please say something Dad!" she pleaded, tears streaming down her tender cheeks.

Suddenly she felt the phone being pulled sharply from her hand, her mother looking down at her furiously whilst terminating the call.

"I told you not to call him again!" Her mother hissed at her, her face set in a piercing scowl. Her mother always spoiled things for her …

She hated her mother. She was always Daddy's little girl, conspiring against her mother with him in hushed whispers, sly looks and hidden laughter that she made sure her mother could hear. She hated her mother taking her away from her dad. But she wasn't going to give up trying to get what she wanted, she always got her way in the end with her dad.

Every time she managed to escape her mother's censorship, she would call her dad. It didn't matter what time of day, she knew he wouldn't mind. Unlike her mother, his love was unconditional. She could bend him to her will at ease. Her mother was always an obstacle to her plans. She wished she could just be with her dad, no one else.

At first when his daughter had started calling him secretly, he wouldn't speak with his whisky addled mind inhibiting his voice and propelling him in alternating waves of hallucinations and lucidity. In his half sober moments he would sob at the sound of her voice and hang up abruptly as his heart felt like it was breaking in two as he listened to how she wanted to be with him so badly.

"You've got to stop calling me, sweetheart," he said eventually.

"Why Daddy? Don't you love me anymore?"

"No! Of course I do! I always have, always will," his reassurances came through tears.

"Then come to me, take me away from here. I hate it here!" she said in a hardened tone. It was the closest she could get to stamping her foot at him in person.

"I can't …" He broke down and shook violently with the emotional pain. He had sacrificed so much for her, but this was too much, even for him.

"It's my fault you and Mummy aren't together again, isn't it?"

"No! It wasn't your fault that we're not together any more … you must never think that …"

"Then why did she take me away from you? Please let me live with you! I promise not to be naughty again, ever, ever, ever!" She was almost screaming at him now, frustrated by his pathetic attempts to placate her.

She had learned early on that emotional blackmail often got her what she wanted. When her parents were still together, she would accuse him of working late so that he could avoid reading her a bedtime story, despite him begging her to understand he needed to work the long hours to pay the bills and buy her the things she wanted. She would scream at him that she hated him. That normally resulted in a 'guilt' gift from him the next day.

"I HATE YOU DADDY!" she finally screamed. She

heard him let out a short cry and the phone went dead. She knew she was slowly breaking him down and that soon she would get what she wanted. She smiled at her own genius.

It was only a few weeks later, after more persistent phone calls from her, that he finally said, "Guess what sweetheart, I've found a way to come to see you. We're going to be together again soon, I promise."

She smiled, and said, "Come soon Daddy! I can't stand it here without you!" and sobbed a bit for effect.

Eventually he appeared in front of the mother and daughter, smiling sadly as the family was finally reunited.

The shock on her mother's face was priceless when she saw him!

It was almost the same expression her mother had worn when she had frozen in shock as the oncoming car shrilled its horn at them in fear and urgency ...

She had planned to get rid of her mother, and the crash had all been part of the plan, except it backfired. At school it had been drummed into them that seatbelts saved lives, and if you didn't wear one, you could get killed. She had wanted her mother dead in what would look like an accident.

She had distracted her mother by screaming at her in the car when they were driving home from the shops and started having a tantrum about not getting the game she wanted. Her mother tried to stop her thrashing and in the commotion didn't notice her daughter had unclipped the seatbelt in the driver's seat.

As limbs wrestled with each other, her mother didn't realise their car had slid onto the other side of the road. There was no way the oncoming car could have stopped in time.

She hated being stuck here in purgatory with her mother, it was only her mother who was meant to die.

"WHAT HAVE YOU DONE?" cried her mother now, hands to cheeks that were flushed with horror and rage.

The girl just smiled, she always was good at manipulating her father. She had known that it was only a matter of time before he would take his life to join her. Now she could control him in death as she had in life, and she missed having that feeling of power over him. She already had plans on what she would make him do from this ethereal state. The girl smiled again at her own genius.

THE SHADOW

"HE CAME AGAIN last night." Betty said matter-of-factly.

Her daughter elbowed the granddaughter in the ribs as the latter sniggered. Her daughter laid a comforting hand over the paper thin skin of Betty's clasped hands. "You were probably just dreaming, Mum. They are giving you some tablets to help you sleep."

Betty smoothed the blanket over her knees. Her joints ached constantly, but at 88 years of age she couldn't expect to be sprightly. It seemed the older she got, the more people talked down at her, dismissed her claims, began to treat her like a child. Everyone seemed to know what was best for her, except for her.

"I know what I heard. There were footsteps outside my door. A heavy man's boots walked down the corridor and stopped right outside my door. I went to open the door, and no one was there." Said Betty adamantly.

"You couldn't have walked to the door, Mum, you need someone to help you out of bed. So you see, you must have been dreaming," her daughter said soothingly.

Betty remained silent, fuming in anger but unable to express her frustration. Finally she said, "I'm tired now. I think I might go back to bed."

After she had been transferred to the bed, she heard her daughter and the nurse talking at the other end of the room. They thought she couldn't hear, but she heard snatches of conversation revolving about dementia. *They are wrong,* she thought, *I may be slow but I am of sound mind. I know what I heard.*

Her days were mundane. The care home tried to provide activities, but Betty felt she was not among equals. The other residents weren't stimulating company, and flower arranging wasn't really Betty's idea of a fun afternoon. The television wasn't very engaging either. Betty couldn't concentrate very well any more. She would sit in her room and reminisce of her life, her regrets. It seemed her happy memories were suppressed in the recesses of her mind.

Some days later, she woke again to the sound of thud … Thud … THUD! Those boots again! Stopping right outside her door. She could hear heavy breathing.

"What do you want?" she shouted at the door, although her vocal chords were unable to produce much noise. The breathing continued, almost mocking her. "What do you want?" she cried again. Suddenly she heard running down the corridor. A night shift carer entered her room, slightly breathless. "Betty! What is it?"

"That man! That man was outside my door again!" said Betty, flustered.

"There's no man here. I just came down the corridor, there was no one here but me." The carer added, "You must have been dreaming."

Betty allowed the carer to fuss over her and pretended to sleep to get rid of them.

Days passed uneventfully. Betty contemplated death. It wouldn't be long now before she found out whether she had followed the true religion, or if there was no afterlife. On one hand she accepted death, but on another she was frightened by the unknown.

Then it came again at night. That rhythmic thud moving down the corridor and stopping outside the door.

This time she heard the door handle turn, and the door creak open, but the man didn't enter. Betty lost her nerve and remained perfectly still, too scared to move. She knew it was futile to mention it to anyone. It was a relief when the carer came to do the hourly nocturnal check on her.

Betty wondered who the man could be. He wasn't the spirit of her husband, as her husband had never worn such noisy boots. She couldn't think who it could be? Her dad maybe? That seemed equally unlikely.

More days passed and Betty was woken again by the footsteps. Incrementally, the intruder was becoming bolder. She would hear the boots walk down the corridor, stop outside her door, enter her room, and it felt as if he just stopped and stared at her. She never actually saw him, just felt his presence. She lay petrified, until finally the carer came to do the hourly check on her.

Betty grew more distant from her family. She didn't like the way they laughed at her. If they were going to mock her, there was no point in confiding in them. Her daughter tried various schemes to stimulate Betty, but Betty steadfastly refused to engage in any activity. Her body was tired and she struggled to concentrate.

Finally, the day came when the intruder followed his usual routine, but this time as he entered, he walked straight to her bed. Betty stayed frozen still, petrified, silently begging the carer to come in. She felt the mattress depress next to her as the intruder lay down in the thin space between her and the edge of the bed. Betty was petrified at what he might do to her! Instead, he whispered so closely into her ear that she could feel his breath.

"It is time …" said the deep voice, simply.

And with that, she felt an arm curve around her waist, gently pulling her body against his, and as she touched his ice cold skin, she felt the life within her being sucked out, and finally realised the identity of the booted intruder.

AUGUST

RED MOON

RESURRECTED

A FIGURE DARTED in and out amongst the headstones, only her lamp could be seen from afar, bobbing up and down like a will-o'-the-wisp.

At last she found the grave that she sought, sank to her knees and placed the lamp next to her.

"Robert, my love, it has been a week now and you have not come to me!" She started scrabbling at the earth, pushing it aside. "The magic woman promised you would return to me in three days, but all I see of you is a shadow of yourself in my dreams, every night, a shadow of yourself. And Robert, my darling, you look at me so angrily! Why? Why, my darling? I was promised you in the flesh and instead you plague me with your look of anger, all I feel is anger from you."

She clawed at the earth frantically, breathless in her endeavours. And then she heard the breathlessness of another. She gasped and turned around in mounting terror … could it be …?

"Annie!" Her brother was bent double, gasping for breath. "I saw you leave the house at this late hour and followed you. What are you doing here? This is no time to grieve at the grave! Why are you disturbing the earth? You cannot be planting flowers at this unearthly hour!"

"John, dearest brother!" she sobbed, pleadingly. "Don't be angry with me! I can't live without my beloved Robert! We were cleaved at the heart, I have lost my soul with his. So I went to the magic woman and paid her what little I had left. She performed a ritual and promised me he would return to me in three days, but it's been a week now, John, and I have seen nothing of his return! I must know if the grave is empty, perhaps he is lost, perhaps he cannot remember his way back to me …"

She saw the look of horror on her brother's face. He grabbed her shoulders angrily and shook her. "You consulted a magic woman? You committed this act of ungodliness? Do you not see you have condemned his soul to hell?"

"To love someone to your dying breath is not a sin!" she cried back in anger, pushing him off her. As he stumbled back and lost his balance, he fell on top of the grave and was suddenly struck by a horrifying realisation.

"Wait here!" he commanded. She looked on as he scrambled up and ran into the distance. Presently he returned with a spade and started digging.

"Dear Brother, you will help me then!" she said, relieved and hopeful.

"This is not for you, Annie! This is for Robert!" He shouted angrily. He couldn't bring himself to tell her the darkest thought that had entered his mind.

She watched him silently pummelling the soil out of the grave, until at last he felt the spade slam into the coffin. He cleared the soil off the lid and prised it open with the spade. Annie cast the light of the lamp over the coffin. The light first illuminated the scratch marks on the underside of the top half of the lid. Annie moved the light across to the corpse. There lay Robert, face contorted in anger and helplessness, hands clenched and raised to his chest where he had frantically tried to claw his way out of the coffin.

"Nooooooo!" screamed Annie. "Nooooooooo ... She never told me I had to open the coffin! She never told me you would return alive in the coffin!"

HONESTY

MY HEART LIFTED as I heard the familiar percussion of heels against tiles. I knew the rhythm: it was my wife Jean coming to visit me. When you are rendered immobile, speechless and sightless in a coma as I am, you become fine-tuned to sounds that you would otherwise zone out as background noise. I heard the nurse tell her in the corridor that the doctor would like to speak with her. I enjoyed listening to Jean sobbing for me. I had never had so much attention from her since we first began dating. She was easy to flatter back then and once I had committed her to me through marriage, I began to improve her by telling her how to dress, behave, how she should spend her day, and other life skills. She became sullen, but of course she was too well mannered to show her anger in public.

I didn't much care for her thereafter, so long as she continued to play the attractive wife, I could get relationship fulfilment elsewhere. I didn't mind if she spent my money on clothes and meals with friends, so long as they were friends and meals that I approved. After all, I was the breadwinner, I was the managing director of a manufacturing company. I wielded the power. And yet ironically, here I was, trapped in my body, powerless.

As I mentioned before, I enjoyed this newfound attention from Jean, but I was aware that the true reason for her tears were actually from worries as to what would happen to her if I died. I made sure to tell her that she would get nothing in my will, and I was smart enough to get her to agree to a pre-nuptial agreement. I refused to let her work so that she was totally financially dependent on me. I like to keep my assets secure.

The nurses saw her as a devoted wife and she played along to that. Duncan, my business partner came in once or twice, probably for show. I heard him whisper to Jean, comforting her. I would put a stop to this relationship as soon as I was released from this medical prison.

"Don't worry," I heard Duncan say, "I will always look after you. And then silence, with just the whisper of something intimate – had they kissed? – and then the hum and regular beeps from the machines keeping me alive came back to fore. Inside I was writhing in anger. Outwardly I must have looked asleep. I started plotting my revenge. I didn't sleep as such in my coma, I just drifted in and out of darkness. I had no idea how long each period of darkness lasted, so time was unknown to me, there was no way for me to know how much time had elapsed in between the bouts of being aware of my surroundings.

Today Jean wasn't sobbing. I didn't hear the scrape of her chair so I knew she was standing over me. I smelled her perfume get stronger as she leant over me, her breath hot on my face, the scent had citrus undertones, so not a perfume that I approved of as I always believed that a woman should smell of sweet flowers.

She put a hand over mine and gripped tightly before whispering bitterly in my ear, "Goodbye, Seth, I hope you rot in hell."

She raised herself up and in her normal tone said, "I am ready to see the doctor now."

What did she mean about hoping I would rot in hell?

A short while later, I heard multiple footsteps in my room, much talk in low voices, and then the din of the machines stopped. There must have been a power cut. I fell into the darkness again.

The machines were still silent when I emerged again from the darkness.

I heard footsteps approach me, familiar rhythm, but I couldn't place the person. There was also something different about the sound of the steps, more muffled than they'd been before. An unfamiliar texture to them, nothing like the clipped noises of shoes against tiles in the hospital. "Well Seth, the money got the better of you." It was my younger brother David, who had always been jealous of my success and author of many failed startups.

The footsteps receded, and then another set of footsteps approached me, slightly irregular, as if limping and with that same muffled quality ... My old friend Tim!

"I'll have a dram of whisky for you, Seth, I'll miss you. Have a safe journey." I heard him sob a little. What did he mean have a safe journey? I pondered as he also walked away.

Then, "Goodbye Mr Grantham, the office is a lot happier without you. I wanted you to know that." Why, my young clerk Williams! I felt the anger swell inside of me. Wait till I got out of this coma, I would make him pay, or not pay him as the case may be. Then followed a stream of people, mostly members of staff, gleefully lining up to tell me exactly what they thought of me. This was torture! I endured all the insults by the ungrateful cretins whilst planning how to exact my revenge.

Finally Duncan stepped forward. His was the most cutting statement of all: "It's all mine now, your company, your wife.... All those times you overruled me, undermined me, threatened me, and yet here I am, the victor."

My hate for him intensified to a degree I didn't know I was capable of feeling! If that wasn't bad enough, I then heard Jean's footsteps approach me. She stood next to Duncan. I felt something land on my hand, prickly and velvet at the same time.

"He doesn't deserve a rose," I heard Duncan say.

"I have to play the part of the grieving widow," sighed Jean. There was a pause, and then I heard a clattering noise above me. Why was my bed clattering? It sounded like a metal object striking wood.

"Are you sure?" asked Duncan.

"Yes, "replied Jean firmly. "He can take his wedding ring to hell with him. Don't worry, no one will notice, I am wearing gloves for the rest of the day."

Wedding ring? Why was she throwing that at me? She couldn't seriously be thinking of leaving me for Duncan?

Speak of the devil ... "Have you thought about what you will do with the ashes?"

Ashes? What ashes?

"I though the park where he had many of his assignations would be ideal. I like the thought of me scattering his dope ... I liked the thought of scattering him there, and the dogs ... fertilising the earth with their waste."

Both stifled giggles.

"The crematorium is nearly ready. We should go," said Duncan as they walked away. The word became embossed in my mind: *Crematorium*. Why would I be at a crematorium? I wasn't dead after all, I was just in a coma.

Jean? Suddenly it dawned on me as to what was happening.

Jean! No! I'm still alive! Alive I tell you!

THE SPELL CONSULTANT

JENNIFER WATCHED discreetly through her kitchen window as the saw the woman in her business suit – not the polyester kind it seemed – struggle to walk down the front garden path. She was trying to avoid brushing against any of the overgrown plants, scowling at any attempts nature made to caress her as she strode past. Jennifer smiled to herself. She enjoyed watching the business obsessed types being annoyed by her plants in her cottage garden, where nothing was neatly cut or pruned so as to encourage as much wildlife as possible. They would appreciate nature one day, and realise just how synthetic their own lives were.

The woman couldn't find a bell, so she briskly rapped the brass knocker which was appropriately shaped like an upside-down horseshoe. The door opened almost immediately to reveal a middle-aged women dressed in an oversized white shirt, a colourful thin scarf and what looked like a handmade skirt.

Jennifer smiled warmly at the woman. "Ah! You must be my 2pm appointment!" Her smile faltered as she watched the woman look her up and down in disdain, as if it would be lowering her standards to enter the house. Jennifer ushered her in, "Come through to the kitchen, we will conduct our business there," and led her down the corridor, inwardly wincing at the clatter of the woman's heels on her natural wooden floor. She didn't understand why women obsessed over heels when they were so uncomfortable to wear. She preferred her collection of Doc Martin boots in punky designs with their comfortable soles. She suspected the woman disapproved of such unladylike footwear, but that also gave her a small satisfaction.

The kitchen was large with farmhouse type cabinets, copper pans hung on the wall and herbs hung on wooden racks suspended from the ceiling. There was an Aga, and a kitchen dresser with shelves filled with glass jars with handwritten labels – they appeared to contain various seeds, plants and crystals. The window overlooked yet another overflowing garden. Probably the woman was thinking that she could clearly not afford a gardener.

"Please, have a seat," Jennifer gestured towards a wooden farmhouse style dining table. "Can I make you a tea or coffee?"

"Do you have any Lapsang Souchong tea?" asked the woman, as if that was a common tea that people would have in their cupboards.

Jennifer suppressed a smile. "I'm afraid not. I only have bog standard black tea, I'm afraid, will that be OK?"

"Well, if that's all there is …" The woman settled uncomfortably into a chair.

Jennifer boiled the kettle and pulled out a large teapot and two stained, chipped mugs to gain extra disapproval from the woman. She decided that bringing out a plate of jammy dodger biscuits would be taking the class wars a little too far. She listened to the woman ramble on, desperate to fill the silence in these disagreeable surroundings.

"I've never met a witch before, you're not what I expected, well … I don't know what I expected really … I don't normally do this kind of thing, I don't believe in … it's just that … well, one of my clients strongly recommended you. He said you changed his life."

Jennifer suppressed another smile – it was that particular client who had arranged this appointment, asking Jennifer to help this woman more for his sake than for the woman's own sake.

"How does it work exactly? I tell you what I want and you cast a spell for it to happen?" The woman was struggling to withhold a note of scepticism.

"Not exactly. You need to be aware of the Rule of Three," explained Jennifer patiently. "Whatever you ask from the universe will be returned to you threefold. If you wish harm on someone, harm will come to you threefold. If you do good, you will receive goodness too, threefold." Jennifer brought over the teapot, mugs with sugar and milk on a tray to the table. "I only have oat milk, I hope that's OK."

For a split second the woman squirmed and then re-composed herself. "I think I'll take it black," she said, spooning in extra sugar after Jennifer had poured her a mug.

"Now, tell me about yourself. Firstly, how would you like me to address you?" asked Jennifer, finding relief in her own mug of tea from the strained atmosphere.

"I am Mrs Macbeth," she smiled proudly.

Jennifer smiled back at her, indulgently. "And what is your real name?" Coming to a witch with a name like Macbeth was like checking into a hotel under the name Smith. People found it funny to give her a pseudonym after the famous Shakespeare tragedy. The number of times she heard jokes around 'Double, double toil and trouble; Fire burn, and caldron bubble …'

"Oh, that is my real name!" The woman sounded affronted.

Jennifer gave a slight nod. "And how is it that I can help you, Mrs Macbeth?"

"My husband and I run a beauty products business. It's a family run business with his brother and sister and their partners. Unfortunately my husband's siblings aren't as ambitious as he is, and are holding us back from expanding the business into something more profitable. I need you to cast a spell to enable us to buy out the other stakeholders and run the company ourselves. We have the potential to grow the business into the global market …"

Jennifer let Mrs Macbeth rabble on about her ambitions for the company. She realised this woman was a dominant force in her marriage, and in the board room, and was almost as ruthless as her Shakesperean namesake.

"I see," said Jennifer at last, after Mrs Macbeth had released her greedy ambitions and sat back, arms folded in satisfaction. "Well, let us see how the universe can help you. Please remain seated whilst I prepare. Help yourself to more tea." And with that, Jennifer stood up and proceeded to gather various items. She lit candles and incense at the table. She brought out crystals, started pulling herbs from the bunches suspended from the ceiling, seeds and other plants form the jars on the dresser.

"You're not getting an eye of newt or legs of frogs are

you?" Mrs Macbeth asked, feebly attempting a joke. The woman really couldn't tolerate silence, or loved the sound of her own voice, or both, thought Jennifer.

"No. I'm vegan," said Jennifer matter of factly. Mrs. Macbeth looked at the oat milk in front of her in despair.

Jennifer brought over the herbs, an empty tin can, some parchment paper and a pen.

"I am going to write your intention on this paper, and then I will repeat some spells and burn the paper with some herbs, and as I chant the spell will be cast. I need you to meditate on your wish whilst holding onto these crystals," she passed Mrs Macbeth a couple of small polished stones.

"Just meditate on your wish," Jennifer repeated and started chanting something so softly that it was inaudible.

"What is it you are saying?" asked Mrs Macbeth, intrigued.

"If you interrupt the spell will be broken. I will let you know when the ritual is over," Jennifer said sternly, and started chanting again.

She wrote something on the paper, rolled it up and put it in the tin. She chanted continuously whilst waving crystals over the plants, putting some plants in an empty glass jar and the rest in the tin. She added smaller crystals to the glass jar, sprinkled some essential oils onto the contents of the tin and lit a match and set the items alight whilst maintaining the incantation. The smell was acrid, pungent, woody. Smoke arose in great plumes, Jennifer captured some of the smoke in the glass jar and sealed the jar quickly.

Mrs Macbeth watched, mesmerised. It all felt surreal. Jennifer fell silent for some moments, concentrating on the tin, and then looked up at Mrs Macbeth and said, "It is done."

Mrs Macbeth released the crystals from her hands. "What happens now?"

"You need to perform a follow up ritual for the next thirty days. Take this jar." She handed it to Mrs Macbeath, in which she had added herbs and crystals and captured some smoke. "And light a white candle next to it every night. Ask the universe to guide you in achieving the intent of the spell. You will see results after that."

"And what is the success rate of your spells?"

"It is very rare that they don't work. It depends on the person's commitment to the spell."

Mrs Macbeth felt a shift inside her body, almost imperceptible, but something had definitely changed within her. She felt as if she was not quite in her body. She took the bottle, gathered her things and left the house feeling as if she was in a trance.

Jennifer felt her shoulders lighten at once after Mrs Macbeth's departure. She returned to the kitchen to make a fresh pot of tea, then slumped back on her chair and let out a low groan. How much longer would she have to entitle herself a 'spell consultant' and perform these sham rituals? It wasn't that she wasn't a witch – she was a proud white witch – but she did deceive many of her clients by pretending to cast a spell for their wish, but instead casting a spell for the goodness in that person to triumph over their greed or ill thoughts. Her incantation for Mrs Macbeth was to cleanse her soul, not grant her power. She had done something similar to the client who had booked this appointment for

Mrs Macbeth. That client was a changed man, and could see the error of his ways, and could see the errors that could be corrected in Mrs Macbeth.

Jennifer looked around the kitchen. She grew tired of having such an old fashioned kitchen and old crockery. She wanted a fresh, clean, white and stainless steel kitchen with an elegant plain white modern tea set. She was tired of objects overcrowding her line of sight, all these herbs, copper pans she never used, the fussy design of the kitchen cabinets. Oh how she would love to re-style her home in some neutral shades, white walls, barely any furniture, like a Scandinavian minimalist home! Instead she had to live up to the image people expected of her, otherwise her business wouldn't flourish.

One day, she thought to herself, she would perform a 'Swedish death cleanse' and be able to be her true self.

SEPTEMBER

HARVEST MOON

UNWANTED GUEST

"THAT'S THE LAST of the boxes," panted the removal man, cursing the four flights of stairs and no lift in the block of flats. Camilla thanked him and his partner, and paid them the money owed, plus a small tip for their efforts. She wanted to be rid of them as soon as possible.

"Nice view of the city from here!" The removal man seemed to only just notice the main selling point of the flat. Camilla didn't want him to linger and offered to see him out. As soon as she had ushered out both men, she shut the flat door and slumped against it in relief. She wanted silence, peace and time to meditate. The unpacked boxes and unarranged furniture seemed to look at her reproachfully. She would deal with them later. She would pull out the essential items (wine and bath salts), unwind with a drink and bath and look forward to her new life in a new city. She wanted to put the past firmly behind her and make this the fresh start that she needed.

A sharp rap at the door jolted her out of her daydream. It must be the removal men, they must have forgotten something. She opened the door reluctantly but was met by a woman in a leopard print top, black leather skirt and peroxide hair piled high in a furball mess. The woman gave her best friendly smile, revealing nicotine stained teeth.

"Hello, love! I saw you just moved in and thought I would come and say hello!"

Before Camilla could respond (although in truth she was tongue tied), the woman marched past her, took a slow around the open plan kitchen and living area. "What a fantastic view of the city!" exclaimed the woman to herself.

Camilla finally found her voice. "Yes, it's what drew me here in the first place."

The woman suddenly seemed to remember Camilla's presence. "Oh don't mind me, love, I'm ever so nosy," she said brightly. "Love looking at other houses. Can't get enough of all those moving home programmes on TV! I'm Adele by the way. I just wanted to give you a proper welcome here. I live further along down the corridor, number 9, always around if you want a chat!"

In contrast to Adele's enthusiasm, Camilla couldn't think of anything she would rather not do right now. "Camilla," she responded, nervously.

Adele looked at her strangely, then looked over her shoulder and back at Camilla. "Is everything OK?" she asked, wondering why Camilla kept staring past her. "Is there someone else here?"

Camilla looked startled for a moment, and swallowed hard. "No, just me. I'd offer you a drink but unfortunately I've not had a chance to unpack." She hoped this was enough to encourage Adele to leave.

"Oh don't worry love, I thought you wouldn't have had anything unpacked, I saw the removal men had just left, so I thought I would help you settle in with this," and with that, she pulled out two small cans of Bacardi and coke from her handbag and a packet of cigarettes and sat down on one of the kitchen stools.

"Oh," she said brightly as she spotted something poking out from one of the boxes, "I see you smoke too!"

She pulled out the small clay dish and lit up a cigarette.

"Actually I don't," Camilla corrected her, "That's for incense."

Adele ignored part of the response and carried on blowing out smoke. Camilla opened a window, she was too tired to engage in an argument.

"Incense? Well I prefer scented candles myself. I find incense a bit too bohemian myself." Adele laughed to herself and opened her can. "Don't you want any?" she asked Camilla, who was looking increasingly distracted.

Camilla looked at her blankly and then sat down opposite her. She reluctantly opened the can and took a small sip whilst eyeing Adele, who in turn began to feel uncomfortable. This was an odd woman. She wasn't quite here, in the present.

"How long have you lived here?" asked Camilla, trying to break the awkward silence.

"Eight years, love, seen lots of people come and go. Unfortunately a lot of people I knew have left and most of the flats are now short term rents, so there's a high turnover of tenants. Are your renting then?"

"No, I bought this place." Camilla seemed reluctant to look at her. Adele wondered if she was on drugs of some sort. She couldn't maintain eye contact and kept looking at something else beyond Adele herself.

"Where did you move from?" Asked Adele, determined to get some personal information out of Camilla. Why was Camilla alone? Had she broken up with someone? Adele liked to know these personal details.

"Just the other side of the city. I wanted more space." Camilla wasn't giving much away. She still kept looking at Adele's shoulder rather than her face. Definite weirdo, this one. Adele suddenly felt drained of energy and didn't want to hang around someone who wasn't conversational.

"Any kids?" Adele asked. Camilla shook her head, almost sadly.

"I've got three myself, they almost cost me a remortgage!" She laughed at her own perceived witticism. Camilla smiled weakly at her and quickly looked down.

"You don't talk much, do you love?" Adele stubbed out her cigarette.

"It's been a long day with the move," replied Camilla carefully.

Adele stared at her suspiciously, but then broke into a grin. "Well I should let you get on with that task. If you need any help, you know where I am! I hope you're very happy here!"

Adele got up to leave. Camilla thanked her for coming and for the drink and saw her out, watching her tottering expertly in heels down the corridor. As soon Adele was out of sight, Camilla again shut the flat door and for the second time that afternoon slumped against the flat door and slunk to the floor with her head in her hands. How could it have happened so quickly? She had sensed the energy as soon as Adele had walked in. Then the energy had materialised into the entity attached to Adele. It was definitely a mischievous entity at best, but in Camilla's experience, most were evil. She wondered how long Adele had had the entity attached at her shoulder. The air in the flat now felt unclean, and not just from the cigarette.

Camilla stood up and with a heavy heart she walked over to a box marked 'altar'. She pulled out sage sticks and crystals and incense. She had been forced to leave her previous flat because of a spirit that only she could sense, and who wished her harm. She didn't want to risk Adele's entity transferring to her. She would have to perform a cleansing ritual and protect herself from Adele. She had only just moved here, she didn't need any more unwanted guests, either in human or spirit form …

NO HIDING PLACE

THE WAVES RIPPED and sprayed against the rocks, and the boat pulled away in time before the monstrous sea claimed another victim, the silhouette of the boatsman diminishing into the rapidly fading light. The boatsman had sped away like the devil himself was after him!

Klaus suddenly felt a deep sense of fear and loneliness as he leant forwards into the wind, trying to steady himself against the rocks which seemed to slither beneath his feet as the weight of his backpack crushed his shoulder blades.

He wondered again if it was a good idea to come to this remote island, far away enough from civilisation to be insulated from the comforts of technology. There would be no phone mast here, no access to emails, social media or television. He would be lucky to pick up a signal from a transistor radio. It was just him and nature, and hopefully the few island inhabitants he hoped to find. Now that he had actually set foot on the island and felt its menacing air, slow pricks of doubt pierced his mind: had he done the right thing?

He had always wondered about his father and as a child played out fantasies with a fictitious version of a dad who would teach him skills to survive in the wild, kick a ball with him after school and take him sailing from one island to another across the North Sea. But as it was he only had a hazy memory of a thin figure with dark rimmed glasses, clutching a leather briefcase as if it was more important than life itself. His mother refused to talk about his father, or his mysterious disappearance, she would become tight lipped and then change the subject. She would rather leave the room than discuss where his father had gone before he disappeared. He only knew that his father was a historian doing some research on the links between his Nordic island homeland and Scottish islands. There was a conspiracy amongst the family too about his father, as family members would diplomatically avoid discussing the absence of a brother/ cousin/ son. Klaus grew up surrounded by whispers, although none of this sinister dialogue was disclosed to him.

Finally, when his mother left the mortal plane to face whatever fears she had of the realm of the dead, he had finally found a clue to his father's last destination in amongst her papers. A hastily written note to her with a crude map to indicate the island to where he was heading. Klaus had been coming to Scotland for several years now trying to determine which of the remote islands harboured the secrets of the last movements of his father. Unfortunately he was not a skilled sailor like his father and so was not able to sail on his own to the islands as his father had. Instead he would use local boats and ferries that made routine trips to the islands, or in this case, charter a boat when all others made clear their refusal to come anywhere near this island! The boatsman he finally managed to persuade to take him was in need of money to feed his alcohol dependency, and Klaus wasn't sure if it was the addiction or fear that compelled the boatsman to take regular gulps from his hip flask as they made the crossing.

The inn where he had chartered the boat had fallen silent

when he asked about this particular island. Then one old islander spoke and practically spat at him: "'Yer bum's oot the windae!" The other islanders muttered in agreement as they followed the old woman out. Only the boatsman had stayed on and offered Klaus a ride to the island for an extortionate sum of money. Klaus had wanted the boatsman to come back in two days to collect him – the island was only a mile wide and a couple of miles in length so there were not going to be many inhabitants and Klaus was prepared to pitch up his tent for that time. The boatsman eventually agreed but on condition that if he did not see Klaus at the pick up point at 10am on the agreed date, the boatsman would not even moor up before turning round and heading for home. Klaus was sure he could stick to that arrangement. The boatsman seemed so anxious that he wouldn't even tie up the boat at the landing bay when they arrived – he expected Klaus to jump off onto the rocks and then the boatsman made his hasty departure.

So here was Klaus, as isolated as the island itself, trying to navigate his way through the damp, knee-high grass to find somewhere suitable to settle down for the night. As if to make him feel further unwelcome on the island, storm clouds gathered like hounds to their prey, and with a seismic roar of thunder, hell opened its gates to throw a downpour that could almost sink the island!

Klaus staggered on, blinded by the rain, barely being able to look ahead. There was a proverb in his country that there was no such thing as bad weather, only bad clothing. If that was the case, Klaus thought, then he was as ill equipped as someone climbing Everest in shorts and a t-shirt.

Just when he thought he might sink into the mud beneath him and never get up again, he saw a short distance away a familiar looking circular white building with a black slated roof. It was a church! Just like the churches in his own island! This church could be his saviour, quite literally!

He felt reignited with energy and bounded through the field onto the tarmac path leading up the church. There was a great old oak door above which were a row of small windows that appeared to be blacked out. Klaus lunged at the door expecting to find it locked, but to his surprise it was open, and his momentum threw him across the threshold into the vestibule.

Dazed, and with the weight of his sodden backpack crushing his lungs, he looked up to see the bottom of a black robe floating peacefully in the breeze that had accompanied him in. His gaze followed the line of the cloak upwards leading to a white collar, where a man with a benign face, hands clasped in front, said with a kind smile, "Welcome to the church of lost souls!"

Klaus scrambled up and relieved himself of his backpack. He started rambling in a flood of words that almost became coherent, trying to explain his arrival on the island and his need for shelter. The pastor patted him on his shoulder and gestured for Klaus to sit in one of the rear pews. The church was not as small inside as Klaus had first imagined, and had a mezzanine level with seating. Klaus fleetingly wondered how such a small island could have so many inhabitants as to warrant a church with such a seating capacity. The windows behind the altar were covered in a black cloth, also an unusual feature.

The Pastor went to the altar and poured some wine into a golden goblet and returned to Klaus. Klaus noticed how the Pastor always clutched the cross around his neck with one hand, whatever he was doing, almost like a comfort gesture.

The Pastor smiled again as he handed Klaus the goblet, "Here, drink this, it will warm you up. We get the occasional stray tourist here, and you are most welcome to stay here the night." He gestured to the altar. "I was just preparing for our service this evening. It is the Harvest Moon tonight and we have a thanksgiving service for the bounty of food this island provides, we call it the 'Harvest of Lost Souls', as we have so many committed members of the church.

Klaus felt some warmth flood his insides with the calming effect of the wine, and placed the goblet beside him as he unpacked a towel and began to dry himself off.

"Thank you for the offer of letting me stay," said Klaus. "You have no idea how thankful I am. I am not sure I could have put up a tent with this wind and rain! But I don't want to interfere in your service, you must tell me where I should put out my sleeping bag, out of the way of the congregation."

The Pastor laughed at him in a friendly way and patted his shoulder again. "No! No! You must stay here and join the ceremony now that you are here. I am sure as a tourist you will find it most fascinating! But what brings you to this humble island?"

Klaus took some more wine before he tried to explain himself. He gave a brief history of his quest, and explained how this island was one of the last possible places where he could trace his father's last movements. The Pastor closed his eyes and had his hands clasped in front of him again. He seemed to be meditating, or thinking deeply.

"What was your father's name?" he asked eventually.

Klaus told him. It was the name of one of the oldest families to reside in his home island.

The Pastor smiled and nodded his head. "Yes, I seem to remember that name! A young serious looking man, always clutching his leather briefcase for dear life! He was in fact right in that there is a link between his home island and this island!"

Klaus sprang to his feet in shock.

"What! You knew my father! You need to tell me everything! I need to know what happened to him!"

"Stop, my friend!" laughed the Pastor. "All in good time. I will tell you everything after the service. Come up to the front with me whilst I make the final preparations. The congregation will be here at any moment."

Klaus asked the question that had been playing on his mind since he had sat on the pew. "This church seems awfully large for such a small island! Do you really have so many inhabitants?" The Pastor turned to smile at him again, "Oh yes! We have people who come from far afield to attend our services."

"But the islanders where I stayed before didn't even want to talk about this island!"

For the first time the Pastor's eyes narrowed into what looked like a flash of anger. "Those islanders are the victims of superstitious nonsense that has been inbred in them for generations!" He smiled again and regained his composure and began smoothing the purple velvet runner along the altar table.

"I wasn't expecting to find a round church here, I thought they were only on my island! Until I went to another Scottish island and found a round church there also."

"And do you know why the churches on your island are round?" asked the Pastor as he arranged some unidentifiable accoutrements on the velvet.

Klaus was beginning to feel queasy. Perhaps the excitement of finally discovering the island which was his father's last known destination, the rough crossing or an amalgamation of all the events of his journey to this point, were taking a toll on him. He steadied himself against the altar table. "On my island they were part of the structure to provide a defence against military attacks. But on the other Scottish island I was told that the church was round so that there were no corners where the devil could hide ..." Klaus felt his speech slur ... he lost his grip with the table and began to sway back and forth.

The Pastor smiled at him again. "Oh, but I am not hiding!" He released his hand from the cross to reveal the cross was upturned. The black shrouds of the windows fell at once and in the dusk Klaus could see rows of headstones in the graveyard beyond, but there was something not right with the scene ... The headstones were also upturned crosses.

Confused and unsteady, and now barely able to speak, Klaus stretched his arms out to the Pastor for help. "You ... Drugged ... Me..."

But the Pastor now grinned menacingly, his once amiable eyes now glinting red.

"We do in fact have strong links with your family, which your father tried to break ..." The Pastor grabbed hold of

Klaus as Klaus felt his knees buckle, and swiftly placed him on the table in one eloquent movement.

"Generations ago, we were betrayed by a member of your family who tried to extinguish the church and congregation. I do not take kindly when my followers are burned to a crisp. I used to have living souls come here to worship me, and your ancestor confined them to the spirit world. So now with every new generation, I take the firstborn son from one of your family members. They all end up here in one way or another …"

Klaus couldn't move at all now, he could barely breathe. He saw shadowy figures materialise in the pews of the mezzanine.

"Your father was the last to come here. He thought he could get rid of me with some spells, holy texts and holy water that he carried with great care in that battered leather suitcase of his. But he met the same fate as his forefathers."

The Pastor placed a cup next to Klaus's rigid neck, and produced an ornate dagger from beneath his cloak.

"I used to have living people worship me here, until your ancestor broke rank and turned to the other side. Now I just have the lost souls of the congregation who all perished in the fire."

Klaus could see the shapes on the mezzanine more clearly now. Men and women in black, the men with long scorched beards, misshapen eyes where the flesh had melted. The women wore black caps and black dresses, their faces also disfigured.

And in amongst this sea of grotesqueness, Klaus saw a familiar figure: a young man with thick black rimmed glasses and with an expression of immeasurable sadness as he watched his only child slain in sacrifice at the altar, blood being collected in the goblet, the bounty of food on this island for the harvest of lost souls.

OCTOBER

HUNTER'S MOON

GODCAKE

"EEEEEEEEEEEGGGGGGGGHHHHHHHHHH!!!!!"

The silence of the windless night was pierced by a high pitched screech that could have woken the dead. In fact, that is exactly what it did …

Moonbeams illuminated the Godcake, the triangular section of the road, now covered in grass, where carriages once turned around. Now retained as a historical feature, few people knew its other purpose: the place where witches, thieves, suicides and vampires were buried, so that should they rise, they would be confused and not which way to turn from the centre of the Godcake, thus trapped in the triangle. An eternity of frustration for the sins that they had committed.

"EEEEEEEEEEEGGGGGGGHHHHHHHHH!!!!!"

This time the screech had risen another octave, the earth trembled, the soil crumbled and bodies pushed through the grass.

"EEEEEEEEEEEGGGGGGGHHHHHHHHH!!!!!"

The final scream was enough to lure the bodies from the frost bitten ground. The banshee, the entity responsible for the screams, floated to the Godcake, satisfied that her All Hallow's Eve alarm call had raised the bodies trapped beneath.

Every year on this night, the dead grouped together for a brief release from the prison below ground. A tall striking man in a tweed suit and cravat brushed himself down until he looked presentable. He inhaled the chilled air as if he was inhaling the scent of an exquisite wine. It was just for show. In fact, he couldn't smell anything, but he loved the opportunity to display some flamboyancy.

He smiled as a familiar figure approached him. "Thank you, my gracious lady, for releasing me again." He said in a cut glass English accent, and gave a faint bow towards the Banshee. The Banshee giggled like a schoolgirl, and her long, dark straggly hair that had gone through centuries without combing or washing, fluttered flirtatiously despite there being no wind.

Out of all of them, the Banshee liked him the best.

"Your beautiful sonorous voice is a joy to me every year," continued the man, as his eyes became bloodshot and his fangs grew in excitement. The banshee goggled and looked away in embarrassment.

"Sonorous tones? That musical wench damn near blows my ears off every year!" said another man, rubbing his ears and shaking his head to get the high pitched screech out of his head. He was dressed in rags, shirt hung open, trousers torn below the knees, barefoot but oblivious to the cold. The thief amongst them. The Banshee scowled and was about to scream at her highest pitch when a hand clamped her mouth shut to arrest her revenge, and a voice beside her said, "Ignore him, Bertha!"

It was the witch, known as Cat. A beautiful face, pale as the moon, with delicate features which stood out against her black dress. She shone in the moon rays like a beacon in the night. Her hair was like that of a raven, reflecting hues of black, iridescent green and blue. She turned to the thief. "Shame on you McCollins! If it weren't for Bertha, we wouldn't get woken every year and have a chance to taste freedom, even if only for a few hours in the After Moon."

The thief turned to the Banshee and said mockingly, "I'm sorry, Bertha. Your screams are like nightingales in chorus on a summer's night."

The Banshee missed the sarcasm and gave a victorious smile with her blackened teeth.

A cackle interrupted the moment of peace. "You always were a mischievous stoat, Ed McCollins!" said a shrunken, wizened old lady in a black cloak. The archetypal witch in the party.

McCollins bowed his head in mock reverence. "Oh how I've missed your graceless charm, Old Mother Mallard," he quipped. The old lady cackled again.

"If it's not bad enough being cramped up against you all underneath a bloody Godcake all year round, then it's worse to be above ground with all your bickering," said a maiden with her common way of talking. She adjusted her corset, trying to make her dumpy frame more alluring, flicking wisps of knotted hair from her face.

"Ah, Lucy! You look as ravishing as the first day I tasted you!" said the well heeled man. The Banshee scowled at his turn of affection. Lucy put her hands on her milk maiden hips and said angrily, "Lord Carrington! Had you not the temerity to bite me, I wouldn't be stuck in this damned hole with a bunch of beggars and magic women!"

There were gasps from the others, but Lord Carrington, in the true style of his class, merely adjusted his cravat and said soothingly, "Madam, one has to feed …"

A few voices started speaking angrily at Lucy but Cat's gentle voice rose above them and said 'You're right Lucy, we shouldn't bicker on the one day we can roam the earth. None of us wants to be trapped beneath this triangle of doom."

"And remember child," added Old Mother Mallard, "It be us magic women you turned to when you was feeling poorly!"

"I'm sorry," Lucy said, humbled, and then frowned. "Since when did we have a zombie join the party?" Everyone followed her gaze. There on the horizon moved a figure in a zig zag motion, stumbling, swaying, arms stretching out and then jerking back, head lolling … Then they noticed the wine bottle, and realised the motion from the arms was an attempt by this drunk man to steady himself.

He approached the group with drunken cheerful ignorance. "Well blow me! A Halloween fancy dress party! Can anyone join in?"

Astonished faces stared at him in silent response. The drunk swayed unsteadily and ignored the silence. "I got a little confused walking home from the pub. I'm just …" He gave a short hiccup. "… Merry!" And he laughed at a joke only he understood.

"We can smell your merriment," muttered McCollins under his breath. Cat elbowed him in the ribs sharply and he gave her an annoyed glance in return.

"So … can anyone join the party?" repeated the drunk. "I mean, I'm not dressed for the occasion, but I love your efforts!" He pointed at McCollins. "Can't believe you are dressed in rags in this weather! Respect, man, for looking like a real beggar!"

McCollins clenched his fists, which caught the eye of Cat who put a restraining hand over his.

The drunk then turned to Bertha. "Look at that hair! You must have been dragged through a bush backwards to get such a mess of head like that!" Bertha looked at him as if she meant to kill him. Her mouth opened like a portal to hell but Old Mother Mallard managed to cover it with her bony, withered hand before any demonic sounds could emanate from the cavernous emptiness.

"You!" said the Drunk to Old Mother Mallard. "Your make up is awesome! You sure look like a real ugly hag, and that wart is a masterpiece! Hope it's not there for real!" He tugged at it absent-mindedly. Old Mother Mallard froze in shock at his audacity, scowled, and then broke into a gap-toothed smile. "Well thank you sir, for the compliment!" She cackled, and the drunk gave an inebriated giggle, enjoying bonding with the group.

"You, Madam," he slurred, pointing his bottle at Cat, "are one of the finest looking goths I have ever seen!" Cat felt McCollins fist tighten further. She smiled politely and said, "You are too kind, sir." She bowed her head slightly in false gratitude. The man returned the gesture with an exaggerated bow himself.

"And you, sir," he said, addressing Lord Carrington, "look the business with those teeth! How did you get those eyes though? They seem to glow red? Are they contact lenses? You look like a posh bastard if ever there was one!" The drunk laughed heartily.

Lord Carrington's glowed a brighter shade of red in

anger. He stared at the drunk, then leant into him, nose to nose. "My good man, I don't just look like a posh bastard, I AM a posh bastard!" He hissed at the drunk. Everyone held their breath, the tension was palpable. The drunk stared back, shocked at this unexpected response, and then both men burst out laughing. "You had me going there!" said the drunk. The tension dissipated into relief.

Finally, the drunk turned to Lucy. "Wow! That's a magnificent pair of breasts!" He saw her look aghast, her buxom bosom flushing red in anger and almost ripping apart the corset as it heaved in horror. The drunk realised he had said something wrong but couldn't put his finger on what he had said out loud that should have stayed firmly between his ears. If only his mind wasn't so fuzzy. He hiccupped, and the jolt to his head sparked the intelligence he needed.

"I meant dress! That's a magnificent dress you're wearing!" Everyone waited with baited breath to see if his back pedalling would work. Lucy's stern features composed themselves into a more serene expression. Several breaths released in unison. Lucy crooked an elbow as an invitation for the man to take her arm. "Perhaps you would like to join me for a bite or two? You must be hungry after walking for so long!"

The drunk's eyes widened in glee and greed as he took her arm. "That's a most generous offer, Madam! But I have nothing to contribute …"

"Nonsense!" She smiled and squeezed his arm, but did not lead him away. Instead, she turned around to look at Lord Carrington, and said conspiratorially, "After all, sir, one has to feed …"

Lord Carrington smiled back at her appreciatively, but

before either vampire could claim their annual feast, the drunk pulled himself out of Lucy's formidable arm, and said, "You need to feed, and I need to pee ... back in a second!"

And off he walked to a nearby copse of trees whilst giggling to himself. He was vaguely aware of the strange looking party shouting something after him, but he couldn't hear properly what they were saying, something about being trapped in a cake. They must be playing some drinking game. He picked a tree with a thick trunk against which he relieved himself, and as he zipped himself up, he was overcome by tiredness and as he tried to walk back to the party, he fell flat on his face and into a peaceful slumber.

Just a short distance away, a group of ghouls looked across the road. Outwith the perimeter of the Godcake, and therefore out of their reach, lay a sleeping man who was unaware how a call of nature had saved him from a fate worse than death.

WEREWOOF

In Eastern European folklore, a cat jumping over a grave can turn the corpse into a vampire, and vampires can shapeshift into cats.

PELAW THE COCKAPOODLE touched his nose against window and gauged the temperature. The night was bitterly cold but not cold enough to put him off his mission. He wasn't one to back down from a challenge. Behind him there was a dinner party going on hosted by his pet humans. Dinner parties were normally a rich source of crumbs for him to hoover up dutifully, but tonight there was something so intriguing that even morsels of gourmet food couldn't entice him away.

The Black Menace, as Pelaw had named the neighbourhood black cat, was in the garden, slinking around like a stealthy shadow, creeping in and out of the bushes. The Black Menace was Pelaw's nemesis, his arch enemy – their mutual dislike normally ended in a vocal match. The Black Menace had particularly luminous green eyes with an almost equally luminous black coat which was groomed to perfection. The Black Menace would occupy the back garden when Pelaw was absent, leaving a trail of its malodorous, distasteful, scent around what Pelaw considered his territory. The Black Menace existed to be defeated, and Pelaw knew he would be the victor one day.

But tonight there was something different taking place.

The Hunter's Moon was casting its moonbeams into the garden giving the foliage a silvery silhouette. Pelaw watched The Black Menace striding purposefully around the garden until it reached a particular spot beneath some thick foliage. At first the cat pushed earth away, and then sniffed around. Pelaw released a low growl and prepared himself for a full volume warning. Then The Black Menace stood with an arched back next to the spot, and suddenly leapt across the dip he had created. Pelaw could stand it no longer. He belted out a series of guttural warnings for the cat to leave his territory. The cat glowered at him momentarily and then sprinted away.

Pelaw's pet humans reprimanded him for disturbing their dinner party, and he was guided out into the garden. He needed no encouragement. He traced the cat's fresh odour around the boundary to see what the cat had disturbed. He reached the patch of earth over which the cat had mysteriously and inexplicably jumped. The scent of decaying, composting foliage and leaves mingled with The Black Menace's scent, but there was another decaying smell, one that Pelaw couldn't identify. Was The Black Menace trying to bring up a dead animal? The useless cat wasn't even capable of catching a live animal!

Pelaw started digging at that spot. He sensed he was being watched. he looked behind him and found The Black Menace sitting on the brick wall watching him with what looked like amusement. Pelaw growled at him, the cat hissed back.

Pelaw wasn't going to waste time chasing the cat away, he had to unearth the decaying object before his pet humans dragged him inside again.

He flung earth behind him in a determined manner, the putrid scent growing stronger the deeper he dug. At last he felt something solid. He nudged his nose against the object … yes! This was definitely the cause of the odour! He pulled out the object with a hefty tug. A bone! An old bone at that. Pelaw debated whether it was worth gnawing at, given it had such a distasteful stench.

Then something truly miraculous happened: Pelaw sensed a presence. He looked across to The Black Menace. The cat was not the cause this time; in fact the cat had switched his pose so that he was ready to flee at a moment's notice. No, the presence was around Pelaw. Then a mist enveloped him and he couldn't even see the end of his nose. He barked in frustration. The mist grew thicker and formed a vortex. It drifted, and then changed into a human form!

A young woman in a white frilly dress, dark hair cascading to her waist. The Black Menace relaxed and jumped down to greet the woman by purring and rubbing his head against her leg. Pelaw remained rooted to the spot, mesmerised.

"You Clever Cat!" cooed the woman. She was deathly pale but her lips stood out starkly, almost the colour of blood. Her eyes were very like those of a cat, and her hair was as lustrous as The Black Menace's fur. *Was there a real connection between the two?* pondered Pelaw.

The woman picked up the cat and rubbed her cheek against the cat's, dropping gentle kisses upon its head.

"It's been so long since I was here!" said the woman. Her brows puckered in concentration like she was trying to remember how she had ended up in the garden.

Pelaw sensed danger. He didn't move. He needed to see what happened next before deciding how best to protect the pet humans.

"This house used to be a funeral parlour!" exclaimed the woman. "Yes … I remember now … I had been bitten and I was lying in my coffin … I woke up when the morgue beautician tried to embalm me."

She laughed at the memory. "I caught him off guard and he was going to be my first feed, but he managed to stab me with his knife when I lunged at him."

Her hand went to her left breast subconsciously at the memory – Pelaw noted the position. Now he knew her weak spot.

"He must have buried me here in the garden," she said sadly. "I have lain here for decades, but my beautiful friend has raised me once more."

She nuzzled her head against The Black Menace again. Then she spied the people dining inside the house. She licked her luscious lips.

"I'm so hungry …" she murmured.

The Black Menace jumped out of her arms and retook his position on the brick wall. He lay down languidly and thumped his tail in anticipation. This was going to be entertaining …

Pelaw let out a low growl. He knew his pet humans were in danger, but he didn't know how he could defend them. This creature didn't smell like a human. She smelled of death and decay. She made his hair stand on end, and he had the urge to run as far away as he could from her, but he stood firm against his instincts as he had his pet humans to protect.

Pelaw growled again and the woman snapped out of a hungry trance. She looked down at him and said softly, "I can't go for the humans inside the house just yet, I can't afford to attract attention. No, I will start with you! Although you are more of a snack then a meal, but you will do as an appetiser."

She laughed at him, and bared her fangs. He growled at her more ferociously, and not to be outdone, he bared his fangs back at her.

Then the fight ensued: The woman tried to scoop him up but he jumped through her arms and ran behind her. She tried to catch him but he was too quick for her each time. The Black Menace looked on with great amusement. The woman became angry, her eyes yellow with rage, she hissed at Pelaw. He saw her eyes narrow, her back arched and she seemed to shrink into herself whilst her hair wrapped around her body ... She had morphed into a black cat.

The Black Menace perked up his head at this interesting turn of events, while the Vampire Cat and Pelaw circled each other, spitting, growling, screeching mingling in the air.

The atmosphere was thick with growls and hisses. Then the Vampire Cat leaped onto Pelaw, scratching and clawing through his fur, trying to get to his neck. Pelaw in turn scratched with his paws and teeth, trying to find the weak spot she had pointed to in human form. Blood was drawn on both sides. The Black Menace couldn't work out who was the victor ... until both cat and dog pulled apart, breathless with exhaustion.

The Vampire Cat sank down. With a shudder, she morphed back into her human form. The woman's dress was torn, her hair bedraggled, her pale skin covered in crimson cuts and scratches – and a prominent bite mark just below her left breast.

Pelaw braced. She didn't move.

She stared at the stars and her body dissolved into nothingness, just the bones remaining as evidence of her existence.

The Black Menace grunted in contempt at this outcome, and marched off to find some other nocturnal entertainment.

As tired as he was, Pelaw knew he must bury the bones back in their place before the humans called him in. He pushed the bones back in the hole he had created, and filled the void back in with the discarded earth. He had saved his pet humans! He swelled up with pride …

A few months later, as the Cold Moon fulfilled another lunar cycle, Pelaw was again looking out of the window. This time the garden was filled with fairy lights to celebrate Christmas, illuminating some shrubs, intensifying the darkness where the light didn't fall. Behind Pelaw, his pet humans were engaging in mirth and merriment with friends.

A month after that, on another full moon night, Pelaw lay snuggled up between his pet humans in their bed, as was his custom. The wife was stroking his head soothingly and then looked startled.

She turned to her husband and said, "Don't Pelaw's eyes look a bit strange to you?"

The husband turned Pelaw's head towards him. He was met with a pair of bloodshot eyes, and the top fangs were longer than normal. Pelaw gave out an uncharacteristic, menacing growl …

BLOOD MOON

"WHAT PERFECT WEATHER for Halloween, a blood moon!" exclaimed Harriet, as she and her date, Tom, stepped out from the restaurant into icy chill of the evening. The large red sphere slipped into darkness behind clouds and a fog began to unfurl around them.

"Mmmm ... perfect weather for watching a scary movie." Tom winked at her.

Harriet smiled. In fact, she hadn't stopped smiling for the past few weeks since she had met Tom through an internet dating website. She had always scoffed at the thought of meeting someone over the internet, but when her own long-term relationship had collapsed, she had succumbed to trying it out for herself. After a few non-starters, she had finally met Tom and was almost in disbelief at how much they had in common.

She had already checked the viability of his surname *Stone* as her new surname should they ever get married. 'Harriet Stone' had a nice steel edge to it she thought, she rather liked it.

Harriet had always been a lover of ghost stories, and old-fashioned ghost movies where it was the suspense and your imagination that frightened you, not blood and gore. So she had been thrilled when Tom had confessed to enjoying black and white films with the wonderful use of shadows to create an eerie atmosphere. Harriet had suggested that he came back to her place that evening to watch the classic early vampire movie *Nosferatu*. She was a little nervous though as this was the first time Tom was coming around to her apartment. She wasn't very confident at the dating game, and had to steady her nerves a bit over dinner with perhaps a little more red wine than she should have.

Tom linked his arm through hers. "My mother used to tell me that the fog is actually when the spirits come together and walk on Earth, looking for people they remember from their past."

"Really? Well, it's lucky I have you here to protect me from any malicious spirits who are after me."

Was it her imagination or were his fingernails a tad long? Harriet shook her head, she put it down to the wine and her overactive imagination.

"And what makes you so sure that I am not a ghost? Or even a vampire? After all, you have only ever seen me in the evenings, never during daylight hours," Tom pointed out.

"That's true," conceded Harriet (although she was hoping that he would be staying the night and that she would get to see him in the first light of the morning!) "But you can't be a vampire as you had garlic during the meal this evening."

"Actually I tried to be polite and not have anything with garlic in," said Tom. Damn! Thought Harriet, she could only hope she had had enough red wine and coffee to remove any traces of garlic from her meal.

"Well, I can see your reflection in the shop window," she remarked smugly. It was a faint reflection, as the fog seemed to become thicker. Was it the fog affecting her vision, or did he seem to have more pointy ears than normal? Harriet shook her head again, she must be thinking too much of the *Nosferatu* character from the film. She was definitely a little tipsy.

"Nighttime is the only time that you do get to see a vampire's reflection," smiled Tom.

"Well, I must admit I hadn't heard of that before despite my copious knowledge of the undead." Now his teeth seemed a little pointy! *Get a grip of yourself,* Harriet thought to herself, *stop imagining things that aren't there.*

"Knowledge that you have only gained through fiction books and movies," Tom pointed out. They had reached her flat.

"True. But as I don't own a cross, I have one last test I can perform. Vampires can only enter a house if invited in … well, maybe I got that from a film too, but that's neither here nor there. So I therefore do not invite you into the flat. However, if you do cross the threshold then it will be proof that you are not a vampire." She opened the flat door, and then stood behind him defiantly.

Tom laughed and entered the flat, and she followed him. "There!" she said. "So you are a mere mortal after all!"

She started to slip off her coat, and offered to take Tom's jacket. But when she looked at Tom, there was something different about him. As he handed over his jacket to her, she noticed the hair on his hands had become thicker, and realisation came too late when he said to her, "It's not the vampires you should be afraid of …"

The clouds parted to reveal a full moon, and a satisfied howl could be heard coming from the flat. As darkness engulfed her, Harriet had a fleeting thought of just how similar to 'Tombstone' his name was.

NOVEMBER

FROST MOON

THE SCRYING GAME

"RIGHT!" CRIED THE GUIDE with a great flourish of his black cloak, "What have we here? Fresh victims for tonight!" The flock of tourists laughed good naturedly. "And where are ye all from?" asked the guide, pointing randomly at a couple.

"We are from Brittanny," replied a man.

The guide sucked in his breath. "The French! We're at war with the French! I'll be keeping a close eye on ye both!" Everyone giggled.

"And you, Fine Ladies," continued the guide, again pointing at a random group.

"We're from Somerset!" cried a couple of the girls at once.

"England? Don't think you're safe here … I don't know which King you support. I'll be keeping a close eye on youse lot too!"

More sniggering.

"And finally! You two. Where are ye from?"

"Pennsylvania, the States," replied a middle-aged woman.

"Americans, huh? Turned your backs on us, went to war with us too. I'll be keeping a close eye on ye turncoats as well!"

People still laughed.

"Seems to me you were at war with everyone," said the American man good naturedly.

"Aye, that's about right. Like Prince Phillip, there's not

a nation we didn't upset! Right! Let's begin the tour!" With another sweep of his cloak, the guide led the group to the points of interest along the cobbled street that was the main road of the town. There were the usual tales of the town fountain poisoning inhabitants with some pestilence, the Mercat Cross where proclamations were made, the diseases that plagued townsfolk …

"… And this plaque commemorates where the witches burned. One of the many sites." The group fell silent as the guide recounted the various forms of torture endured by the alleged women and men of magic. His descriptions of the exquisite pain endured almost made the tourists feel they were living the experience vicariously. A few rubbed their skins where they thought they felt the cut of a knife, the prick of a screw, the scalding of skin. The guide talked with such emotion as if he had experienced the pain himself.

Some in the group flinched in disgust. "He really looks the part," said one of the Frenchmen to his husband. Beneath the black cloak, the guide wore black jeans, black t shirt and hefty black boots. His face was ashen white with indentations of pockmarks. His hair fell past his shoulders in black, greasy clumps.

"Probably a student trying to earn extra money," whispered back the husband.

"Although they tried to eradicate the witches here, a few remained hidden and continued to practice, first in the woods, then then in caverns within the arches of the bridge. A coven still practices there, and tonight I have special permission to take you down there – as the veil between the living and the dead thins under tonight's full moon. "

A few of the tour party shivered involuntarily.

"Great theatrics," commented the American man to his wife.

"I'm not feeling good about this, Frank," confided his wife.

"If you're feeling scared, then the guide is doing his job," smiled her husband, squeezing her hand reassuringly. "We'll leave him a good tip," he added.

The guide led the group to a door hidden in a dark alleyway. Using torchlight, he led the group down some steep steps.

"They could have installed some lighting down here," muttered one of the girls.

"Adds to the atmosphere though," responded one of her friends.

They reached a stone walled corridor with caves coming off each side, closed off with iron bars. Red candles in sconces on the wall lit the corridor. There were symbols in the scrollwork of each sconce.

"What do these symbols mean?" asked one of the Frenchman, pointing to one of the sconces.

"They are for protection. The Witches believed that these symbols held those who entered this scared chamber here, until a witch released them. So if a witch hunter came looking for them, he would be unable to leave without a witch's permission. It was a bargaining tool of sorts. This way …" commanded the guide, his arm indicating the direction to follow.

The group moved gingerly on, peering into each cave through bars. All seemed empty. At the end, they reached a cave lit up by black candles. In the centre was a shallow pit. To one side there was a black velvet cloth draped over something hung on the wall. More sconces with symbols. There were mummers of curiosity and speculation from the group.

"This is where the witches practiced their magic. The other rooms were their storerooms and studies, but it was here that the spells were cast. This pit is where they performed their rituals. It is said that whoever enters this pit will raise the devils. For these witches practiced the dark arts, not the light, and sacrifice was core to their belief.

"The pit is where the sacrifices took place. Would any of you like to enter the pit and raise a devil?"

This time the laughter had a nervous edge to it. Then one of the gang of girls said, "What's underneath the black cloth?"

"That is where the scrying mirror is kept."

"What's a scrying mirror?" asked the American woman.

"A scrying mirror is a black mirror used to show someone their future."

"Sounds like something out of Snow White," giggled one of the girls.

The guide looked at her sharply. "You mock the dark forces?" His face softened and continued, almost flirtatiously, "Why don't you remove the black cloth and see your future?"

She smiled back at him, she could play his game. "OK, I will," And with that, she strode confidently up to the mirror, turned back at the guide triumphantly, and pulled off the velvet in one effortless sweep. There was a pearlescent black mirror with an elaborate scroll in wrought iron around the edge. The girl turned and stared at the mirror, mouth agape, eyes wide open.

"What do you see?" asked one friend.

"Is it a tall, dark handsome stranger?" giggled another. But the girl remained transfixed by the mirror, an expression of shock on her face. Suddenly she spun around, pushed past everyone, screaming: "Let me out!" But upon reaching the metal bars, she couldn't open the gate.

The guide stood on the other side and gave her a lazy smile. "You can't leave without my permission," he hissed at her.

"What did you see?" asked the American man, alarmed.

"See for yourselves!" she screamed in anger, and then fell into a silent sob.

One by one, each member of the group went up to the mirror. Each one gasped in disbelief at what they saw.

"This has to be a trick!" exclaimed one of the Frenchman.

"No! Witches perform magic, they do not perform tricks," said the guide, with a touch of irritation.

Finally, the American couple went up the mirror. In the reflection, they saw the tour group, bloodied and in a pile in the pit. A dark black mass loomed over their bodies. Stunned, the couple turned around, the group was alive and standing. The candles flickered red and cast long shadows of everyone. Then they noticed another shadow appear from the pit, and which quite obviously wasn't the shadow of any member of the group …

YOU DON'T BELONG HERE

A SENSE OF emptiness pervaded the flat. Meredith sank deeper into her plush leather sofa. Suddenly the white walls that had once been so fashionable (a blank canvas on which you can add a splash of colour, said all the TV daytime programmes), now felt like a sterile prison. There wasn't much to look at, not much to distract the mind. On the glass table was balanced a bottle of wine and a much used wine glass. Meredith took another gulp of wine and mourned her previous life. She felt she was invisible. She could feel herself being absorbed into the blandness of her living room with its sparse décor. She used to be someone. Now she was nothing, as empty as her wine glass, which she proceeded to replenish …

A year ago, life had been so different. Meredith had a good job in marketing and a good life in the city, always going to some cultural event, dinner parties and taking several short breaks and holidays every year. The pandemic put paid to that with a violent sharpness that had struck her down mentally. She hadn't realised how lonely she was until all her work and extracurricular activities had been taken away from her during the first lockdown. Working from home felt like being imprisoned, she needed to be around people. Her friends tried organising online events, but it wasn't the same as talking to people in person in a group. Only one person at a time could talk, it felt so restrictive, and it was hard to get in a contribution at times. These events left her more frustrated and lonelier than ever.

Then a few months later she was made redundant. Meredith felt she was descending a dark staircase, not knowing what horror awaited her at the bottom – but knew that there was a horror waiting for her …

The redundancy pay was generous, but it felt like dirty money given the loyalty she had shown the company for so many years. She was a middle-aged woman; who would want to hire her now when so many young upstarts were vying for jobs and brimming with more energy than a nuclear reactor?

After a few days of indulging in wine and bitterness, she had a lightbulb moment one morning with her hangover expression reflecting back at her in the bathroom mirror. She saw crevices in her face where there should not have been, she saw a frown that made her look older than she was, she saw the pathetic face of a woman in her autumnal years who was now faceless, just another victim of the job market. With her job, she had lost her identity. Who was she now?

It was amazing how most of her friends dropped her once she was made redundant, as if she was not worthy of their time. As if there must have been something lacking in the quality of her work for her to be made redundant in the first place. So this was the other life lesson: friends can be acquaintances in disguise.

And then the sad realisation dawned on her. She had been living this life to fit in with other people, to fill the void of being alone, but she had never been comfortable in her own company.

So who was she really?

The pandemic also had the effect of making Meredith more aware of her own mortality. All those new and rarely worn clothes that she was saving for special occasions might not get worn again. What a waste! Right, she thought, I am going to turn my life around before it's too late. She checked her savings account and decided to bite the bullet. She had saved enough for a rainy day, and she decided that now was that rainy day! Meredith had always loved writing stories as a child and harboured thoughts about writing a historical novel, but time was always an issue in her life. Now was her opportunity! She would escape to Edinburgh, a city she always found artistically inspiring, and isolate herself for a month to start on a book. There was no sign of the pandemic ending, so she might as well recharge her batteries before she started looking for work. She found a cheap Air BnB close to the New Town, packed a supply of wine and toilet rolls, and made the long drive up…

The Air BnB flat was in stark contrast to her own: walls painted in fresh colours, a mismatch of second-hand furniture and potted plants and knick-knacks all around. Meredith thought she would hate staying in such a cluttered place, but now each item felt comforting, something to stimulate her visually.

And after a week of discovering a myriad of architectural delights in Edinburgh's New Town, from Georgian houses with wide cobbled streets, to tenement buildings with mottled grey and brown stone against a stark blue sky, unexpected features carved into buildings, stumbling upon quite corners with more modern flats, Meredith absorbed the historical atmosphere which was a stark contrast to the glass and concrete from the hub of the city she lived in.

But that sense of loneliness never left her, no matter what she did to stimulate her senses. She had only a few close friends and no family with whom she maintained contact. She had moved on from the toxicity of family long ago. Friends were her family now, no matter how few she had.

Who am I? She thought for the umpteenth time. She was no longer a successful Marketing manager, that was for sure. A novelist, she was going to be a novelist, just until her next job.

The rain felt more like a wintry monsoon then just a heavy downpour! Meredith's anorak couldn't seem to withstand the onslaught of water and she felt the dampness creep into her flesh, chilling her bones. Typical Scottish weather! She had been prepared for some wet weather but she had never been as wet as she was in her first week in Edinburgh. This trip was meant to help her rediscover herself, instead she felt isolated and empty. Then she saw a light on in a basement shop and through the sheets of water assaulting her, she realised it was a bookshop. Perfect! She would seek shelter there, she could browse books until the rain subsided and she wouldn't need to try to justify her time in the shop, like she might have to in a café.

She heard the tinkle of a bell as she stepped into a dark, welcoming room lined floor to ceiling with books, dark wooden floors and a few armchairs with warm lighting. It felt like a library in a home rather than a bookshop.

"Hello!" said a sonorous baritone voice with great joviality.

Meredith turned to face them, a tall young person dressed in black, with a skeleton mouth face mask, long brown hair and black rimmed glasses. Her memory juddered and she pulled out her own floral face mask.

"If you wouldn't mind putting on some hand sanitiser too …" The person in black pointed to the shelf behind her where there were a couple of pump dispensers of what was now the ubiquitous hand hygiene. "You're soaking wet! Let me take your coat for you whilst you dry off." Meredith was touched by this small gesture. She handed them her dripping anorak whilst they hung it up discreetly behind a door. Thunder cracked above the shop; a flash of lightening caught a badge on their black shirt which read 'Kill Amazon'. Meredith smiled behind the mask.

"Were you looking for anything in particular?" asked the person.

"Well, perhaps some historical fiction. It's been a long time since I read a novel. I have time now so thought I would take up reading again."

"Oh, well we have a few of those! It's always good to make time for yourself," they said jauntily and directed her to a couple of shelves. But Meredith hardly paid attention as she suddenly realised that interspersed amongst all the books were typewriters! They looked like antiquity, but she remembered how her own mother used to have one, and the pleasure of hearing the percussion of the keys with the rhythm of writing. There was a pleasure with using typewriters that a computer keyboard could not replicate. Here there were old metal models, and the less old plastic types that were common in her childhood.

"All these typewriters!" exclaimed Meredith.

"I have the only shop in Scotland that repairs typewriters," said the young person, flicking their glossy brown hair back in a proud gesture. Meredith was impressed, someone as young as this person owning such a quirky shop!

A wave of nostalgia and impulsiveness hit Meredith. "Are these for sale?" she asked. This was what she needed! She needed to feel connected to her writing again. Not through the pixels of a laptop with its soft keys, but with the crude mechanics of a typewriter, and the reassuring noises it would make as she typed, bells ringing as she approached the end of a line, the zipping noise it would make as she pushed the carriage lever to reach the next line. For the first time in months she felt excited! She felt motivated, she felt she had a purpose again.

They looked at her cagily. "Some of them are for sale, some of them I want to keep for myself."

Meredith smiled again. "I think I should like to buy one …"

The person arranged for her to try out a couple of models that she was attracted to, but they seemed to hesitate when she picked a 1920s dark red model with gold embellishments and glass keys. It came with a case which had a delicious scent of old books bound in leather. Meredith inhaled the scent and wondered who the first owner had been?

"Is it not for sale?" she asked.

The person hesitated again. "It is for sale …" they said theatrically, "but it has a curious history. It was first owned by a lady who used it as a scrying device. She connected to the spirits through writing, but sometimes she couldn't write their messages fast enough, so she used the typewriter to transmit the messages instead."

Meredith's eyes danced with laughter; her smile hidden beneath the mask. "That's quite a story! But I'm afraid I don't believe in the supernatural. Once we are gone we are gone. It's a beautiful machine, and I like it best out of all the ones on offer."

The person acquiesced and gave her a quick overview of some of the functions that might not be so obvious to someone not used to using an older model typewriter.

As she finished paying for her purchase, the person asked her, "Frog, shark, elephant or dragon?"

Meredith was a bit taken aback by the question. "Pardon?"

"We give away an origami creature with every purchase," they explained, holding up small origami forms made from pages of old books destined for pulping.

"Oh!" said Meredith, delighted. "I would love a dragon!" Dragons reminded her of happy days in her childhood immersed in fantasy stories.

Meredith left the bookshop feeling lighter, despite carrying a heavy typewriter, and a paper dragon in her pocket.

Back in the flat, Meredith carefully placed the typewriter on the desk in the bedroom. The desk was nudged up against a window and a radiator, so Meredith could look out to the old tenement buildings and array of rooftops beyond. There was a pot plant to one side which made the desk feel welcoming, and a lamp on the other which made it feel cosy. Next to the typewriter Meredith placed her designer notebook and fountain pen. Excitement fluttered in her stomach. She slid in some copy paper into the roller and adjusted it to be straight, and then she typed a few sentences. At first her fingers slipped between the keys, but once she found her rhythm, the creative energy flowed and she rattled out a random paragraph of nonsense but enjoying herself immensely. There was little room for errors, few formatting options and no internet to distract her.

The rhythmic tapping of the keys was reassuring, they signified that she was producing something! She wondered who had owned the typewriter before her, after the lady who used it for her mediumship. Could it have been another author? A journalist? Or was it just for clerical work? Could the energy of the past owners come through the typewriter into her own writing?

This is me, she thought, *I am a writer.*

That evening, Meredith excitedly called her close friend Sarah to update her on her new purchase. Meredith walked around with her phone doing a zoom call with Sarah so that she could show her the typewriter and the flat. Meredith finally curled up on the sofa to continue their chat. It was the first time in months that she felt really alive!

As they caught up on their respective news, Sarah started frowning. "Who's that in the flat with you? I thought you were alone there?" asked Sarah.

Meredith was equally puzzled and looked around. "What do you mean? I am alone here!"

Sarah looked concerned. "But I definitely saw someone walk behind you! It was a man, I am sure of it."

"Stop trying to spook me, Sarah," Meredith laughed dismissively. "You're just trying to frighten me after I told you about the medium using the typewriter!"

"Check the flat ... For me ... Please!"

Meredith sighed. "OK, if it will put your mind at ease ..." So Meredith gave a second tour of the flat whilst opening cupboards that could be harbouring a human.

"I'm sorry, Meredith, maybe it was just a shadow or some technical illusion. I just had to be sure." Meredith reassured her it was all fine, and she was grateful for the concern.

Meredith found the history surrounding her in Edinburgh was just the inspiration she needed to start on her novel. She drafted plot outlines and characters in her notebook first and then developed them on the typewriter. She loved this rudimentary process. She became totally absorbed in her work, the words flowed out easily, and as she became more engrossed she felt like she was becoming part of the typewriter. At some point, she didn't know when, everything became dark, not from the fading light but that sensation of falling asleep in the middle of task. She found the keys pressing on her face and noticed the streetlamp outside streaming yellow light into the bedroom. How did this happen? She had never fallen asleep like this before! She switched on the lamp on the desk and checked where she was in the story. The last sentence read:

"You need to move towards the light."

Why had she written that? It had nothing to do with her story. Maybe she had typed something in her sleep. It was late into the evening. She made a light supper which she devoured whilst watching some documentary about the misfortunes of famous people – not her usual TV choice but mindless fun. She felt the tension escape her shoulders. This break was good for her.

The next day saw Meredith equally absorbed in her typing as the previous day. She would take autumnal walks around the local area to refresh her mind and come back for another blast at the typewriter. Typing was physically exhausting; she couldn't imagine doing it 8 hours a day for work! Working without spelling and grammar checks sharpened her mind more. She loved this process. But then the same thing happened as the night before. She had some music on in the background through a radio app on her phone, and she woke up with her cheek against the keys and with the 9pm news being announced on the radio. Meredith checked the last sentence:

"Get out! You do not belong here in whatever shape or form!"

This was so strange! Was it her subconscious manifesting herself through actions in her sleep? Were these her deep rooted insecurities or bitterness from the redundancy? Puzzled, she repeated her routine of a simple supper and trash TV. But she wasn't paying attention to the TV or the supper, she was too perplexed to concentrate on anything.

The next day she did a zoom call on her phone to Sarah to tell her what had happened. She was on the sofa again with the rain pelting the windows outside, reminding her of the tapping of the typewriter.

Sarah tried to reassure her that it was just a symptom of the shock of the redundancy. Meredith was at the point of being reassured when she saw Sarah's face look puzzled again.

"Are you playing around with the background?" asked Sarah.

"No ... I haven't done that since work."

"You look like you are in an old fashioned room in a large house. There's blue flocked wallpaper and the dining table is round."

Meredith frowned. She could see her image on the screen and behind her was the living room as she knew it with its small rectangular dining table.

"I hope you're not gaslighting me!" Meredith joked. "Everything looks normal at my end!"

"Maybe it's a problem at my end," Sarah said hesitantly, but neither was convinced, Meredith at last losing some of her scepticism.

That night Meredith had a vivid dream. It felt a little unsettling. She felt like a voyeur looking into someone else's life, she felt intrusive. The dream was about afternoon tea being served at a large round dinging table in one of the Georgian Houses in the New Town. There was mahogany furniture and flock wallpaper, there were a group of men in suits and women in loose 1920s attire with flamboyant hats. They dripped wealth. There was a vast mirror above the mantlepiece, and Meredith saw her own reflection amongst the party. There was tension in the room, like anticipation of something fearful about to happen. The tableware was cleared by a maid and the typewriter bought to the table. Everyone sat in a circle around the table and held hands, except a middle-aged lady dressed in black silk who occupied the seat in front of the typewriter. The lady started typing against the dim lights and the silence of her audience. Another middle-aged lady next to her read out what was being written, but Meredith couldn't hear what was being said. In the sharpest of moves, the typist stopped tapping the keys, turned to look at the mirror, locked eyes with Meredith – gasped in horror – and passed out …

Meredith woke with a start, flushed with fear and sweat. Obviously her imagination had got the better of her with the history of the typewriter. She looked across at it – it looked benign. One strong coffee and some toast later, Meredith's nerves were restored. After getting dressed and going out to get some shopping, she was ready for a full day of writing. But as she entered the bedroom she was suddenly struck by a thick atmosphere; it was as if a malevolent presence had engulfed her and the sensation was so overwhelming that she felt suffocated and had the urge to leave the room. As she turned around, she could feel someone directly behind her but as soon as she turned back there was no one there.

She fled the room and sank into the sofa in the living room, switched on the TV and hugged a cushion. She was oblivious to the programme on the TV, she just needed noise around her to make her feel safe. She sat there for a while until she was ready for lunch and tried to rationalise things in her mind. The redundancy must have affected her more than she had realised. But she couldn't face going into the bedroom again. She fell asleep on the sofa with the light on and without getting changed.

Meredith awoke the next morning with a stiff neck and feeling more at ease. She chastised herself for becoming spooked so easily! She tentatively stood in the doorway of the bedroom. There was no atmosphere now, the sun was streaming through, the typewriter glittered in the light. She grabbed a change of clothes, her notebook and pen, and her laptop and made a swift exit. As the day wore on she grew more confident and shrugged off her fears of the bedroom. She was just experiencing strange feelings from her situation, that was all. She didn't write that day, but dipped in and out of the bedroom as she did some laundry and other household chores. By the next morning she was comfortable enough to start writing again. The following days were uneventful but productive. Meredith was brimming with confidence and felt she was achieving something at last!

She continued with her autumnal walks, cherishing the wind biting her face, better than being cooped up indoors. She marvelled at the luminous coloured leaves around her, and treated herself to coffees and hot chocolates in the comfort of the steamed up local cafes. She felt she was excelling in her writing, she really believed in herself.

After one such interlude outside, she came back to the flat and after hanging up her coat and bag, went to the bedroom to slip into some clothes she could lounge in. She was unprepared for what happened next. As she opened the door, she felt her body become paralysed, her hand glued to the handle. She couldn't move at all, but even more petrifying was the sight that beheld her! The bedroom was no longer the bedroom. It was a high-ceilinged Georgian house with blue flock paper and there were a group of people, men in dinner suits and women in silk and chiffon dresses with headbands in 1920s style. They all stopped talking when they saw her, and to Meredith's horror, the woman in black from her dream moved towards her. The woman's face came right up to Meredith's ear such that Meredith could feel the icy touch of her lips against her skin. "You don't belong here!" hissed the woman in a refined Scottish accent with the sound penetrating her senses so deeply that Meredith felt her ear drums would burst. Blackness consumed Meredith again and when she could regain her focus the bedroom had reverted to its normal self, but that thick atmosphere of malevolence prevailed.

Shocked by her experience, Meredith slammed the door shut, grabbed her coat and bag and ran out blinded by tears. She walked briskly and aimlessly for a while, numbed by her experience. Then she found herself back on the street where she had discovered the bookshop. She needed answers. She pushed the door open aggressively, her frustration tempered by a jaunty voice greeting her, "Oh hello! You're back again! How's it going with the typewriter?"

Faced with this normality, Meredith suddenly felt overwhelmed by her experience and burst into tears. The person tried to soothe her, but she shrugged off their words. "Who else has owned the typewriter? I need to know how you got it. Strange things have happened which I can't explain. I need to know it's not just me, I need to know if other people had the same experiences!" Her words tumbled out in a stream of panic. She suddenly felt very foolish. This had been a mistake.

There was a flash of alarm in the person's eyes. "It has had a number of owners over the years, and no one keeps hold of it for longer than a few months. It somehow gets resold back to me, I have never worked out how that happens, and as it's in very good condition, I sell it on again."

Ready for its next victim, thought Meredith.

"Don't worry," she said, "It won't be coming back to you this time!" With newfound determination, she turned around and walked out of the shop and went straight back to the flat.

She started packing up her belongings and carrying them to her car. She felt angry at the events ruining her stay in Edinburgh. It felt like she was being pushed out again, like being made redundant for a second time but in this instance from the stability of the flat. She had noticed a skip on the road and knew what she was going to do with the typewriter.

Once everything had been loaded into the car. Meredith had only one task left. She stood in the bedroom and looked determinedly at the typewriter, hands inside her raincoat pockets. She fingered the paper dragon she had been given when she had bought the typewriter. "Right – I am going to get rid of you. You won't be able to harm anyone else."

She strode towards the typewriter but suddenly she sensed the malevolent presence again. The atmosphere thickened once more, but she fought against it, like trying to walk through treacle.

She reached the typewriter but felt a presence behind her. Before she could turn around to look, she felt her head being pushed sharply against the glass keys. She reached for the table, paper dragon in her hand, try to lever herself upright again against the force, but the exertion was too much. She felt the keys of the typewriter move of their own accord and punch into her cheek. In sheer terror she collapsed …

Her body was found at the end of her rental period, head resting against the typewriter keys, a look of horror on her face. Rather cryptically, there was a page in the typewriter with a single line in the middle of the page which read: "YOU DON'T BELONG HERE!" There was no sign of foul play though. It was assumed the expression on her face was from the heart attack that she suffered.

The landlord didn't want to keep a typewriter associated with a death and sold it to the bookshop known for selling reconditioned typewriters. The landlord could have sworn there was a look of sadness in the shop owner's eyes as they took in the typewriter.

Meanwhile, in another time, in another world, a lady in a loose fitting black silk dress, hair neatly tied in a bun sat at a circular dining table with other guests. Everyone was holding hands except her. In front of her was a typewriter. She typed furiously whilst reading out her words. "You don't belong here! You are in the spirit world! You need to move towards the light!" Her anger and frustration was transmitted through the typewriter. She felt a force resisting her, trying to stop her from typing, but she fought on and tapped the keys more furiously. Suddenly, she sucked in a long gasp of breath and her head fell onto the glass keys of her shiny new typewriter, her hands clutching the table.

When she was revived, she felt something in her hand, and as she uncurled her fingers, she found a strange paper form that looked like a dragon.

DECEMBER

COLD MOON

A GIFT FROM THE MAGI

KIRSTY WOBBLED towards the subway tunnel. She blamed a combination of drink and heels. She had emerged from the pub after having pre-Christmas drinks with colleagues amidst a swirl of last minute shoppers. Her head throbbed with the cycle of festive music that permeated the air, and where masks had once hidden faces, now scarves and hats obscured the identities of the Christmas Eve shoppers. Christmas lights dazzled Kirsty's eyes, and she scuffled past woollen coats and scarves, trying to get to the subway.

Kirsty didn't like using the tunnel at night, but it was the fastest way home. Although there was some lighting inside, the entrance always reminded her of the gaping mouth of a monster, ready to swallow her into the unknown darkness. She had watched too many episodes of Crime Watch …

She shook her head to bring clarity to her mind, focused her eyes and strode more confidently towards the void.

Inside the monster, a thin girl stood by the tunnel wall, a crumpled, stained sleeping bag at her feet, the most precious belonging she had in this world.

"Hello?" she said quietly, as a maelstrom of designer handbags, polished shoes and woollen coats swam past her. "Can you see me?" She spoke a little louder. "Can anyone see me?" she sobbed helplessly, desperately.

People sniffed an unpleasant smell and hurried past her, wanting to escape the bitter cold and return to the comfort of a heated home. Others shot a condescending look towards the sleeping bag and quickly flurried past, not wanting to engage with her. She was a thing to be pitied and loathed, a social parasite, the story of her life. The dangers of being homeless were preferable to the horrors that awaited her if she returned home.

She looked sadly at her sleeping bag. Sometimes she wished the cold would take her, and she could sleep forever, and be safe from the terrors of the street, and the threats of home. The subway was the safest place for her. Outside was full of dangers, like a dragon waiting to devour her.

Then she saw a young woman, luminous against the greyness of the crowd in a white coat, sparkly skirt and equally glam heels. Like an angel emerging from the lair outside. The woman seemed unsteady on her feet, but was briskly coming towards her, looking ahead assertively and not afraid of the people around her. "Hello?" cried the girl more urgently. "Can you see me?"

Kirsty nearly tripped in fright. She hadn't expected to see this almost transparent slip of a girl, thin and undernourished, to come out of nowhere. The other pedestrians pushed past Kirsty as she stood to gape at the girl. Kirsty got over her shock and tried to collect herself. "Yes, of course I can see you."

Oh goodness, she thought, that was a stupid thing to say. Why had she stopped? She normally walked past the homeless with what she hoped was a sympathetic smile. Must be the drink ... She really needed to keep her wits about her.

The girl's pale, drawn face morphed into happiness. "You can see me? You can really see me? Most people just walk past me. I'm invisible to most people. You don't know what it means to me that you can see me!"

Kirsty suddenly felt awkward, normally being one of the people who would normally walk past her. She tried to make light of the situation. "We're all so busy these days, especially at this time of year, that it's easy to miss what's right in front of us." Where did that come from? That sounded so pretentious. Kirsty mentally kicked herself.

"Yes," agreed the girl. "If I had a home to go back to, I would rush back there too. I would want to sit in a warm room, have a hot meal, have a warm bed … I would rush back to all of that too."

Kirsty felt her heart plummet in guilt. She'd normally say that she didn't have change as she used mostly her cards after the pandemic, but then remembered she had some cash just in case of emergencies. She sought out her purse, and extracted three pound coins, shiny brand new, like nuggets of gold. She pressed them into the girl's hands.

"This won't buy you much, but Merry Christmas. I hope you can get a hot drink at least."

The girl looked at the coins in wonderment. She looked up to Kirsty tearfully. "Thank you. You have no idea what this means to me."

Kirsty gave a faint smile in acknowledgement, and quickly walked on before she welled up too.

The girl's gaze followed Kirsty until the angel had safely exited the tunnel. Then she looked down at her own body in the sleeping bag. She pressed the three gold coins into one of the palms of her corpse, and smiled at the miracle: no one had seen her when she was alive, never REALLY seen her, but in death someone had looked into her soul, and given her three gold coins like a gift from the Magi on this bitter Christmas Eve.

As the Christmas Eve Shoppers and revellers continued to avoid the spectre of the homeless, the spirit of the girl lay next to her mortal body and waited for her fate in the next world, smiling at the conclusion of her time on Earth.

G-HOSTS

RAUCOUS LAUGHTER flew out from the small cottage which was bursting at the joists with revellers.

"Mary, will you not drink another toast to your husband?" asked one of the farmhands. Mary sat tight lipped and silently covered her goblet with her hand to indicate she wanted no more wine. No more toasts. Inside she seethed. She wanted them all to leave her be. The more she craved solitude, the more they pestered her.

"Ah, come now, Mary, Jimmy doesn't want you to be sad, do you Jimmy?" He turned to the man sat next to Mary, who looked as stony faced as his wife, looking on vacantly at the festivities before him. Mary couldn't bear to look at him.

Some of the party started playing their fiddles and dancing gaily. Cries of, 'To Jimmy!' erupted sporadically with the raising of goblets.

The husband and wife reluctant hosts did not join in and remained seated, casting looks of disapproval at their guests, feeling more like prisoners than hosts.

One man tried to get Mary up to dance with him, but she gave him her best death stare, and he backed away perturbed.

Mary watched as plates of food were consumed, all at her expense, and the wine flowed freely. Let them eat, drink and be merry, she thought, for it may be their turn next to host the party. Mary stared out of the window, willing dusk to turn to dawn and for the villagers to leave her home. The music, shouting and laughter merged into one distant background noise. Mary was furious at her husband for forcing this event on her. His physical presence repulsed her. She blinked back tears of frustration.

At last! The sky turned a lighter shade of blue. Sunrise was approaching. The laughter diminished, the music and dancing slowly petered out until eventually the villagers filed out drunk and happy, and not without a respectful farewell to Mary and Jimmy, who appeared to be as unhappy as they were merry.

The last to leave was Mary's neighbour, a few years older and many years wiser. She laid a comforting hand on Mary's arm and said, "It's the custom, Mary, we must all endure." Mary glared back at her. The neighbour stepped back and said, "I'll let you two say your goodbyes in private, and I'll be back in a wee while for the last part of the ceremony."

Mary waited until the neighbour could be seen walking across the next field, then she leapt from her chair to the doorway and screamed into the fresh air. She would not look at her husband. She never liked this morbid custom of celebrating the life of the dead before they were buried. She would not turn around and look at the corpse of her husband. She was furious at having to be put through this morbid party as part of the funeral ritual. She couldn't wait for the body to be carried down the coffin path and finally buried.

She stepped outside and shut the door behind her without looking at her husband.

That was her way of saying goodbye.

LUNAR ECLIPSE

BLOOD MOON

BLOOD DONOR

"THEY DON'T OFTEN do this in the evening." The man unbuttoned his cuff and rolled up his shirt sleeve in preparation. He eyed the nurse curiously. She was young but severe looking with a permanent scowl as if she didn't want to be there. Well, he hated working evenings too, and it can't be easy having to do a shift as a single woman in a blood donor clinic in the less desirable part of town. He should be more understanding of health professionals, he chided himself. However, he found women like her a challenge. He set himself a goal to break that scowl into a smile, just a fun, flirtatious game that he liked to play. He was by nature full of optimism and liked to spread happiness where he could. He tried a bit of light humour first.

"I'm not sure my blood would be of any use to anyone. If they got this nectar in their veins they would only inherit my laziness," he laughed at his own joke.

The nurse's scowl deepened. That was good, as the game was not fun if it was too easy. The nurse remained tight lipped with her head down as she prepared the blood bag and needle. "Aren't you going to ask about my medical history?" he asked her. She looked at him with eyes that were almost pools of black, a stare so intense he felt locked in a hypnotic stare with her.

She broke the spell by turning her back to him to collect other items, and said dismissively, "All blood is welcome."

Not a talkative one, this one, he thought, but he found it curious that she hadn't completed any paperwork.

"Is there a national shortage then? Normally I get asked for details."

"None needed." She spoke in clipped tones, still with her back to him, but he found it hard to place her accent. She swabbed his arm, hoping that like most people he would concentrate on her actions rather than look at her face. He did not disappoint. She didn't like them looking at her. She didn't want to be treated as a human. She was no longer human, but she couldn't reveal her true self, so she tried to look away when she had to speak to them so they wouldn't see her teeth.

She tried to identify the vein but it was not forthcoming.

"That vein being shy again? Well maybe I'm not alive, maybe I'm just a vampire," he laughed again at his own joke, still hoping to break through her icy demeanour. He sensed her tense up. Why was she so uptight? She looked at the hollow of his elbow intently. "Quiet please, I must concentrate." Yes, she must concentrate on keeping her hunger in check. She knew perfectly well where the vein was, but she had to act the part. She smarted as she realised as he was concentrating on her face rather than the needle. He noticed her flawless pale skin, the long lashes, drooping eyelids hiding the ebony eyes. She quickly located his vein to stop his gaze upon her. There was a barely perceptible jolt in his arm as she pierced his skin. The way she licked her lips, almost seductively, did not escape him, but he knew the lust wasn't for him. As the blood drew out of him, his attention turned expectantly to the bag collecting the precious fluid. He thought it would be his lazy genes that he would be passing on, but it would be his emotions, memories and knowledge she would acquire through drinking his life force. When the bag reached the required level, she went through the removal process and quickly withdrew the needle and covered the tiny prick in his arm with cotton wool. She didn't want to see the tiny drops of blood, her resolve might fail. It would be like licking the bowl after making cake.

"You may leave now," she said brusquely.

"What? No chocolate or biscuit? Or chocolate biscuit?" One last attempt to weaken her defences. Instead her scowl returned, and those eyes …

"You know, you have the most beautiful eyes, In fact, you would look so pretty if you just managed to smile occasionally." He realised his mistake as he said it. He had meant it kindly but he could see the way her eyes widened in surprise and then narrowed in anger that he had overstepped the mark somehow. It was so easy to offend people these days. She turned his back on him and said sharply, "Leave now!"

He obeyed and made a quiet exit, feeling that he had stirred something within her, but it was not happiness.

She waited a minute so as not to arouse suspicion in case he loitered, and then locked the van door. She sat down with a quality of sadness that only someone of her species would understand. Then she bent over and finally cried discreetly, not wanting anyone to hear. She had not wanted this life – or more accurately – death, but that is the card fate had dealt her. The words of the man rang in her mind. She didn't want to look beautiful. She didn't want to feel attractive, wanted, and all the events that followed those emotions. She didn't want to be reminded that she could have had a partner, could have been a mother, feel the warmth of sun on her skin, watch a sunrise instead of being trapped in the hours after a sunset. She was locked in a purgatory of darkness and a constant thirst for blood. The man had reminded her that she too had been human once. His last comment tore her heart as she remembered the vitality she had felt when she was alive, and that she had never really felt alive until the moment life was taken from her, and now she mourned its loss. Could you grieve for yourself?

She loathed the darkness, she loathed the company of other vampires. She kept a quiet existence, drawing on the skills of her previous profession of nursing to survive. The one element of her human self that had not died was not to cause harm to others. She took the bag of fresh blood, pierced it with her fangs and let the tantalising metallic iron course through her body, which was just a vessel now rather than a part of her.

Happy endings normally had people walking into the sunset together. Hers would be to have the courage to walk into a sunrise.

BLOOD MOON – THE PRELUDE

I KNOW WHEN the clouds are covering the full moon, because they act as an insulator against its potent energy. The darkness within me ebbs and flows like the tide. My senses sharpen at moonrise, and the forces of anger and survival instilled within me during this cycle diminish at moonset. It is when the full moon is at its peak in the sky – or high moon as it is known in my circle – when I really feel my blood racing, when I feel the lust for another's blood, when I feel the unquenchable rage. But it is a slow build up over the hours before I reach this point of transformation.

Tonight is special though, more so than the usual full moon. Tonight is the night of the Blood Moon, where the full is tinged with red, amplifying all my cravings and urges to new heights. I must be extra careful.

I gaze at her over the tealight in its blood red glass holder. I feel the pull of the moon like a magnet shifting my own blood, my urges. I begin to think of blood … No! It is too soon, I must stop thinking of blood. All that is to come later. I feel a shift in the moon's energy … cloud cover, I feel the power within me subside, I begin to relax again. I need to keep control. Not long now until I'll have her trapped.

She lowers her eyelids coyly. She thinks I am being romantic. I don't feel guilty about that, my urges make me lose any sense of compassion.

I order a fish main course when in fact I crave a rare steak. As rarest and bloodiest as they come. But I can't do that, I don't trust myself to keep control. The clouds could part at any moment and my transformation will resume. I can never control when the changes occur, I am at the mercy of the moon.

She orders a beef bourguignon, trying to look sophisticated. And she orders more red wine, more reminders of blood. I smile tightly at her, I hope she doesn't notice. She has drunk a lot tonight, obviously very nervous. If only she realised that she should be nervous, but for other reasons. I feel a sense of power at knowing her fate, the excitement is making my blood rush through me like a sprint race is taking over my body. She looks at my hands tentatively. She's waiting for me to make a move. But I feel the skin on my hands and chest, prickle as the hair follicles begin to enlarge and pulsate, ready to release a think bush of hair across my body. I retreat my hands under the table so she doesn't see the veins throbbing in anticipation, she looks away humiliated. I recover the situation by telling her how beautiful she looks this evening. She looks down, embarrassed. She DOES look beautiful, but like you might find a plate of food look beautiful. I have no romantic notion of *beautiful* with a human.

I let her do the talking. She thinks I am listening attentively. In fact I am trying not to give myself away. I can feel my gums slowly swelling. The less I open my mouth, the less she will see that my teeth aren't what they seem.

I eat my meal quickly, I would rather eject the fish from my mouth. It's disgusting. It has no blood. If I swallow it quickly, the ordeal will be over with soon. Like a bushtucker trial on that famous TV reality show. I hate having to endure this every month, but that is the nature of the beast, so to speak.

I decline the dessert menu but agree to coffee. I don't want to linger too long here. I can feel the power of the moon surge within me, the clouds must have parted again. But I can't afford to let the change take place in public. High Moon is approaching. That's when I suggest we watch a horror movie at her place, one of the many she has in her DVD collection. I pretend I enjoy horror movies as much as she does, but instead the tropes annoy me. She thinks it's a sign that we have something significant in common, like a key performance indicator of compatibility in a relationship. Some prey are so easily manipulated, especially when they have been wounded in the past. I will give them wounds too, but their pain will end, permanently.

I insist on paying the bill. I try not to notice the vein protruding on her neck. My urges are now at the point of being uncontrollable. I feel the pull of the night, the stars, the moon, anger becoming dominant, hunger coursing through me with a vengeance. It takes all my willpower to suppress the emotions and behave like a gentleman, the complete opposite to what I truly am …

As we exit the restaurant, I feel I have escaped a suffocating, claustrophobic coffin.

"WHAT PERFECT WEATHER for Halloween, a blood moon!" exclaimed Harriet, as she and her date, Tom, stepped

out from the restaurant into icy chill of the evening. The large red sphere slipped into darkness behind clouds and a fog began to unfurl around them ...

ACKNOWLEDGEMENTS

OVER THE COURSE of a few years, I would write a ghost story for Halloween and send it out to friends. This book is the product of encouragement and feedback I received from those friends on my writing.

Amongst these friends, I count the wonderful staff at Typewronger Bookshop in Edinburgh for all the support they have given me over the past few years as a local author (do check the bookshop out if you are visiting the city – just a look in will lift your spirits!). A special mention should also go my editor Lorna at Crumps Barn Studio, who acted as my sounding board, reined me in when my imagination went too wild, and without whom this book would not have been possible.

I would also like to give special thanks to my 'coven' friends Tessa and Cat with our shared passion for Halloween, Anne for the use of the writer's retreat in the garden, and Shamal for her inspiration. I would also like to thank Federico for his unending cheerfulness in the deepest recesses of gloom, Wes and my Cherubs for their support from across the pond, Claudine and the Haener Family for providing me with chocolate and standing by me through some very difficult events during the course of writing this book.

There are so many other friends I would like to thank, too numerous to list individually here, but to whom I owe my gratitude and whose friendship I value above all else.

LIMITED EDITION ZINE
produced in collaboration with
Typewronger Books, Edinburgh

Now in selected outlets across Edinburgh
also available direct from the publisher
crumpsbarnstudio.co.uk

ABOUT THE AUTHOR

AMARIS CHASE grew up on a healthy diet of Hammer Horror TV and films, Sapphire and Steel and Victorian ghost stories which fuelled her passion for all things supernatural. Her short stories and poetry have been published in numerous anthologies, including *Spooky Ambiguous (2022), Festival of Cats (2023), The Wild Night Sky (2023)* and *Home Ground (2024). Dark Moon Tales* is her first short story collection.

She currently lives in Edinburgh where she supports her local bookshops, independent cafes (where her stories are often first crafted), stationery stores, and dabbles in book art and painting.

If you loved this book, you'll love these other gothic collections featuring Amaris Chase ...

Spooky Ambiguous

Michael Bartlett, Amaris Chase, Margaret Royall et al.

Ghosts and vampires, zombies and werewolves. A mirror with danger at its heart. A child is delighted to discover she is a witch, and a village disappears under a fairy curse. Then a selkie finds her way back to the waves, before a blood moon rises, bringing its own secrets ... Full of the spooky and the gothic, fairy tales and poetry, this is a brilliant and intriguing collection where nothing and no one is as they seem.

ISBN 9781915067128

The Wild Night Sky

Amaris Chase, Harriet Hitchen, Rebecca McDowall et al.

Stars and planets, vast skies and new horizons. A distant future with secrets in its past. A house sitter intercepts a message from a lost craft, while a tree holds the key to an alien invasion ... and a robot uncovers a lie which may just change everything. Full of mystery and adventure, true memories and poetry, this is a far-ranging collection about our present and future relationship with space

ISBN 9781915067258

Crumps Barn Studio
www.crumpsbarnstudio.co.uk